WL

TROPICAL DREAMS

Nancy should have been spending her holiday in Kenya with her boyfriend, Richard, but only weeks before they were due to leave they had broken off their shaky relationship. Determined not to alter her plans, Nancy had decided to travel alone. On arrival at the hotel complex, she meets the handsome manager, John Norris, who makes it clear he is very attracted to her. Nancy is wary of getting involved with anyone else, but dangerous events on a safari trip are to change her life . . .

CATHERINE RIDDELL

TROPICAL DREAMS

Complete and Unabridged

LINFORD
Leicester

First published in Great Britain in 1998

First Linford Edition
published 2003

British Library CIP Data

Riddell, Catherine
Tropical dreams.—Large print ed.—
Linford romance library
1. Love stories
2. Large type books
I. Title
823.9′2 [F]

ISBN 0–7089–9432–6

Published by
F. A. Thorpe (Publishing)
Anstey, Leicestershire
Set by Words & Graphics Ltd.
Anstey, Leicestershire
Printed and bound in Great Britain by
T. J. International Ltd., Padstow, Cornwall

This book is printed on acid-free paper

1

Nancy bit back tears of frustration, tensing her shoulders and gripping the edge of the counter as she waited at the Hotel Africana Reception Desk. The holiday of a lifetime, planned so carefully and for so long, had started disastrously. Now, she was asking herself, why had she come to Kenya?

A mirror of images flitted through her mind, and tears began to prick her eyelids as Richard's face recurred in the cavalcade of thoughts. He was to have come with her on this holiday but their shaky relationship of the past two years had finally toppled only weeks before they were due to leave. Determined not to alter her plans, she had decided to come to Kenya alone.

She had been assailed by nerves at embarking on such a long journey by herself and her fears had been justified by what had happened at the airport. She kept wondering if the incident would have occurred had Richard been there. Her anger grew, not with the young scamp who had snatched the flight bag from her shoulder and fled but at Richard for having let her down again, simply by his absence.

The airport police and the efficient courier had been courteous and helpful but now here she was, without her passport, return ticket and the various other personal items she had carried as hand luggage on the plane.

'It's lucky your travellers' cheques are in your suitcase,' the courier had pointed out. 'At least you'll be able to enjoy your holiday. Don't worry about the flight home. I'll see that you have a duplicate ticket and as for your passport, I'll arrange the forms in good time to regain entry into the UK.'

The experience had shaken her and she was now fraught with misgivings about the holiday. The interminable filling in of forms and answering questions had taken ages and when the courier had come back to collect her for the last lap of the journey, Nancy had been waiting in the stuffy airport lounge near to desperation.

'Soon have you safely at the Africana,' the courier had said with a condescending smile that made Nancy wonder if she blamed her for what had happened.

Nancy looked around the foyer of the Hotel Africana. The huge ceiling fans whirred rhythmically, gently wafting the fronds of the plants dotted around. She selected one of the comfortable chairs near the reception desk and sank on to it gratefully, waiting for the receptionist to be free.

The coach load of passengers from the flight had continued on their journey, no doubt settled in their rooms, enjoying a hot, soothing shower. The trim figure of the courier approached.

'Everything is arranged.' She smiled. 'Just pick up your key from the desk then I'm sure you'll be glad to get settled. My name is Della Swan. If there's anything I can do, please don't hesitate. I'll see you later in the week when I have everything fixed about your flight home. So relax and enjoy your stay at the Africana.'

Two native boys in maroon uniforms hoisted her cases effortlessly to their shoulders and staggered up the stairs as she walked to the desk.

'Your name, madam, please?'

Nancy's friendly smile matched the broad grin of the young man behind the counter.

'Nancy Evans.'

'Would you please fill in this card? It's for registration.'

Nancy reached for her bag, then, remembering it was no longer there, moaned under her breath as she looked along the counter for a pen. The clerk was answering the telephone.

'Here you are. Use this.'

A young man appeared from behind a cluster of palm fronds. His face was tanned and the front of his dark hair bleached slightly from the sun. He towered over her and when Nancy straightened to look up at him, she found she had to tilt her head to meet his eyes. She smiled as she accepted the pen, feeling her cheeks redden as he casually looked her over, grinning as if in approval.

'Just arrived I see,' he said, bending to glance over her shoulder. 'Ah, Miss Evans,' he added, reading from the card.

Nancy returned the pen and nodded.

'Thanks. Can never find a pen when you're looking for one.'

She blushed again, aware of her trite remark as she handed the card to the reception clerk. He selected a key from the honeycomb of boxes on the wall and pointed across the foyer.

'On the second floor, madam.'

Nancy walked to the lift but before she could press the call button a long slim finger beat her to it.

'Allow me.'

It was the bronzed, young man. They stepped into the lift together and as they stood waiting for the door to close, she felt his eyes on her again.

'I overheard your conversation with Della. Seems like you had a little mishap at the airport. That was bad luck! But don't let it spoil your holiday. Is this your first time in Kenya?'

'Yes,' she said, embarrassed by his persistent attention. 'And you?'

He grinned, showing white even teeth that gleamed like ivory against the deep bronze of his tan.

'I live here. Love to watch the tourists as they arrive looking around, not knowing what to expect. I hear some strange remarks, I might tell you.'

He paused, still smiling and when the door slid open at the second floor he followed Nancy out.

'It's unusual to find a young woman here on her own. Usually it's couples or groups travelling together.'

Nancy felt his remarks invited some explanation but she hesitated, looking at him closely as she fumbled with her room key.

'You seem to be on your own, too,' she said vaguely.

He nodded.

'Why don't we get together later at the bar and keep each other company?'

The last thing she wanted was to be pestered by some conceited, young man who seemed to think she was fair game.

'Perhaps.'

She held the key to the lock and smiled.

'Nice to meet you Mr . . . '

'Norris, John Norris.'

He held out a hand and she felt obliged to give hers in return.

'Perhaps we'll see each other around, Mr Norris.'

'John,' he prompted. 'Yes! I'm sure we shall.'

Nancy nodded, smiling again as she opened the door to her room and went inside. He was still looking at her as she closed the door and seemed disappointed she had left him so abruptly. She shrugged, throwing the key on to the bed and, glancing round the room, dismissed the whole episode.

Her luggage had been delivered and was waiting inside the door. The room was high-ceilinged and airy. Mosquito nets hanging over the bed were tied in a thick knot above the white sheets. Crossing to the windows she opened the sliding door and a wall of warm air tumbled in, almost taking her breath away.

Stepping out on to the balcony, Nancy gasped as she surveyed the view. Her room looked over the green lawns of the hotel that was fringed by a line of palm trees, wavering in the breeze and heavy with coconuts. Tiny monkeys scampered up and down the trees, swinging from branch to branch as they chattered excitedly. Larger monkeys, carrying offspring on their backs and under their bellies, sauntered and strutted on the grass pausing from time to time to look up at the tiered balconies.

'Better keep your door closed,' a familiar voice called from below.

John Norris was under her window, looking up and chuckling. He pointed to the animals playing in the trees.

'They're greedy, little devils, always on the lookout for food. They'll be up on your balcony and into your room like a shot if you encourage them.'

'Right! I'll remember that,' she said smiling then going inside.

It was nearly dark when Nancy left her room to stroll through the garden to the restaurant. The hunger pangs in her stomach had reminded her that she had not eaten for ages, so after unpacking, she made food her first priority.

She'd changed from the beige linen trouser suit she'd travelled in to a cool green silk dress. Fluffing up her bobbed dark auburn hair she eyed herself in the mirror satisfied with what she saw.

The approach of evening had cooled the air and there was a gentle breeze moving the palms silhouetted against the deepening blue sky. Stars were dotted like sequins in the velvet night and seemed to hang over the Indian

Ocean like a mantle. The gentle rustle of the palms blended with the lapping waters on the beach creating a soothing, gentle calm.

'It's beautiful, isn't it?'

She turned quickly, roused by the voice at her elbow. It was John Norris! He smiled as he waved an arm, expansively taking in the sea and sky.

'Really beautiful. There isn't a sight like it anywhere in the world.'

Nancy nodded without speaking. Was this man dogging her footsteps? Had he been waiting here for her? She glanced at him. His white shirt gleamed as it reflected the lights from the restaurant and the cut of his dinner jacket accentuated his broad shoulders. He eased a finger into his shirt collar.

'Still rather warm though. It's cooler inside because of the air conditioning. Shall we go in?'

Nancy felt obliged to do as he suggested though for a complete stranger he was taking control, she thought. This is something I could do without. I've come several hundred miles to escape this kind of dominance. John Norris caught her eye and smiled.

'I hope you're hungry. There's always a great selection of food to tempt even the most discerning palate.'

The maître d'hôtel bowed, as they entered the dining-room, indicating a table set apart from the others. It stood on a raised balcony overlooking the rest of the dining area. Tall, crystal goblets glistened under the lights flanked by an array of silver cutlery and pink napkins folded like flowers marked the two places. As they sat down, several diners waved to attract her companion's attention and when John Norris saw them, he waved in friendly acknowledgement, smiling broadly.

'Lovely bunch of people,' he said. 'It's great to see them enjoying themselves.'

He settled back in the chair and picked up the menu while Nancy marvelled at his condescending attitude.

11

'May I order for you? Your first dinner in Kenya should be memorable and I know you must be hungry after the long flight here.'

Without waiting for her approval, he began to give instructions to a waiter who appeared from nowhere and when he hurried off, he leaned across the table to look at her.

'I must say you're very quiet. Still worrying about your lost bag?'

'A little,' she replied.

His tone sounded patronising and Nancy bristled as she looked at him, forcing a thin smile. He was acting as if she was some waif he had picked up off the beach. She didn't need him to escort her to the restaurant or order for her. She was quite capable of doing that herself. She felt inclined to tell him so but at that moment the waiter reappeared and they were occupied with the array of food.

'That looks great, Djal.'

John Norris nodded in approval and the waiter's face erupted into a wide, ivory-toothed smile.

'Give Mtunga my compliments.'

Nancy looked at him wide-eyed as he explained.

'Mtunga's first in command in the kitchen.'

'Really.'

She picked up her spoon and began to pick at the bowl of fruit in front of her, conscious of his eyes on her from the other side of the table. She felt herself blushing under his scrutiny and when she flashed a furtive glance his way, she was a little disarmed by the warmth of his smile.

'There's a great cabaret later. You'll really enjoy it. All the tourists do.'

Nancy finished her fruit and carefully laid the spoon on the plate.

'Tell me Mr Norris . . . '

'John, please,' he insisted.

She went on, barely noticing his interruption.

'Do you lie in wait at the reception desk for all unaccompanied females and give them your undivided attention like this, or am I being singled out for this very special honour?'

Nancy knew her tone was laced with sarcasm but his attitude had brought out the worst in her and she found it hard to suppress.

'Well,' he began, 'I thought you might like some company being on your own, maybe a little shaken by what happened at the airport. And on your first night here.'

His words trailed as he continued to look at her in surprise.

'I certainly didn't wish to give you the wrong impression, but you could have said no,' he added more firmly.

His jaw tightened and he ignored the waiter who hovered to remove their dishes. He studied a corner of his napkin as he smoothed it between finger and thumb, then looking up at her he shrugged.

'I'll leave you on your own if you wish.'

The words held a question and he waited for a reply.

Nancy blushed furiously and looked down, hoping to hide her embarrassment.

'I'm . . . I'm sorry, Mr . . . John. I sounded awfully rude. I didn't . . . '

He reached across the table and took her hand.

'Then you don't mind if I stay?'

She felt the increasing pressure of his fingers as she nodded, smiling.

'I'm grateful for your company, really,' she added and to her surprise, she realised she was.

'Well, that's all right then.'

He smiled across the table and after a pause said, 'May I ask why you are alone, or would you consider that an intrusion of your privacy?'

When Nancy didn't answer immediately, he leaned forward and added, 'You seem to be a very private person, if you don't mind me saying so. Now you're here, you'll find people are very friendly and won't let you sit on the fringe. So, I'm warning you, be prepared to open up and join in all that's going on. That way you'll have a memorable holiday.'

Nancy listened attentively, wondering how she would cope if she was surrounded by boisterous holidaymakers intent on pulling her into their activities. That wasn't why she'd come here at all.

'Just as long as I have time to be myself,' she said twiddling her napkin. 'I really came to soak up the local colour.'

'Oh, you'll get a good tan,' he began but she shook her head and chuckled as she replied, 'Maybe I will but I meant I want to see as much as I can while I'm here. Perhaps I'll never come again.'

His eyes were warm, reflecting the lights as he grinned.

'That would be Kenya's loss then.'

He continued to smile as he wiped his mouth and Nancy noticed that even the tiny laughter lines on his face were tanned into the crevices.

'Have you always lived here?' she asked.

16

'I was brought up in Nairobi. My father was in the diplomatic service and stayed on when his tour was completed. Can't say I blame him. What is there in London to compare with this?'

Djal loomed at his elbow and leaned between them to place silver tureens on the table. He removed the lids with a flourish then stood back to await the approval that came quickly.

'That looks good.'

John Norris glanced at Nancy who nodded, smiling at Djal's obvious pleasure. He whispered something to the waiter who bowed and hurried away, returning seconds later with a bottle of wine in an ice bucket.

'With the compliments of the house,' Norris said grinning across the table as he filled their glasses. 'I think you'll like this. It's an imported French wine. That's one thing we can't do here in Kenya, make our own wine, though we make a tolerable beer.'

Nancy sipped the sparkling liquid and raised her eyebrows.

'It's lovely,' she said sipping again before setting her glass on the table. 'You seem very much at home here Mr . . . John,' she corrected herself again as he looked at her quickly.

'It is my home.'

Nancy gasped and leaned forward, resting her elbows on the table.

'But, I thought you said you lived in Nairobi.'

'I did, until I went into the Hotel and Leisure Company. I'm the manager and administrator of the Hotel Africana. I thought you were aware of that.'

She sat back in the chair astounded by his words.

'That explains it,' she murmured, her words tinged with the same disappointment that left her with a sickening pang somewhere in the region of her stomach.

Norris bent across the table and peered into her face.

'Explains it? Explains what?'

'Your interest in a woman travelling on her own. I suppose you do all you

18

can to help your guests settle in.'

She blushed as she went on hesitantly.

'I was thinking you had an interest in . . . that you seemed to be . . . '

'Interested in you?' he finished for her and smiled. 'I am,' he said shortly. 'I'm still wondering why you are on your own. You haven't told me yet.'

He began to serve from the silver dishes and Nancy groaned as he piled her plate with a medley of vegetables to surround the filleted fish that almost covered the plate.

'This is delicious. It's a local fish. Tomorrow I'll introduce you to cream of coconut soup.'

'Tomorrow?' Nancy smiled. 'Does this service continue then?'

'But naturally. These are delightful people.' He waved a hand towards the rest of the diners as he spoke. 'But I'm not going to let them monopolise your attention. You haven't come here for silly games around the pool. You've already told me you want to see some local colour . . . well, I'm going to show you some.'

Nancy bit her lip as she gazed across the restaurant. Could this really be happening, she asked herself in bewilderment. She looked at John Norris beneath her lowered eyelashes. He was the most handsome man in the hotel. No doubt about that and here he was promising her . . .

'Come on,' he urged. 'You really must try the fish.'

She picked up the knife and fork and did as he suggested. It was all that he'd said and she began to eat with relish. As the various dishes appeared, carried by the exultant Djal, Norris plied her with food, insisting that she should try everything.

'Evening's the time to eat. Must build up your strength for tomorrow. You'll find it's far too hot to eat much during the day. You'll probably settle for a snack at lunchtime. In fact, I'll see you at the pool cafeteria at one o'clock sharp.'

'Oh, how can you?'

She laughed as his face creased into a frown.

'How can you be thinking of food already when we seem to have eaten enough to feed an army?'

He wiped his mouth with the pink napkin then carefully folded it before setting it aside.

Leaning across the table he said quietly, 'I wasn't thinking of food. I was making sure of seeing you again.'

Nancy blushed at the undisguised admiration reflected in his eyes as he looked at her long and hard with only the glimmer of a smile playing around his mouth. She laid her napkin on the table and began to stand up. John Norris was quickly at her side and rested his arm lightly on her shoulder.

'A quiet stroll in the garden, then I'll take you into the ballroom to see the African dancers.'

He raised his eyebrows, waiting for her approval. Nancy blushed, aware of his closeness. The magnetism that drew her towards him frightened her. She had just escaped from a relationship that was leading nowhere and the last thing she wanted was to find herself engulfed by feelings that could only lead to more frustration. This holiday was to be the beginning of a new life, the start of being a whole person again. She wanted peace and time to reassess her direction for the future.

Norris propelled her gently towards the door.

'It'll be cooler now. Night falls quickly in the tropics and the air's much fresher. You might feel a chill. If you feel cold we can come back inside.'

They were about to leave when the trim figure of a dark-haired girl pushed open the door.

'Ah, John, just the man I've been looking for.'

It was Della Swan, the courier. Her large brown eyes quickly lighted on Nancy. She glanced from one to the other.

'Have you already eaten?'

He nodded and she went on.

'I have a few things to straighten out. I was hoping to catch you at dinner. Can you spare a moment now?'

Her sharp eyes rested on Nancy.

'I hope you've settled in OK.'

'Yes, thanks, everything's fine.'

Sensing the courier's hesitancy, Nancy turned to John.

'I'll go for that stroll in the garden. Thank you for a delightful meal. Perhaps I'll see you later.'

She smiled at Della who returned the friendliness with the impersonal, businesslike smile she saved for her clients. The pleasantry slipped from her face as easily as she had forced it there and as Nancy closed the door behind her, she noticed the girl had casually slipped her arm through John's with the ease of someone who knew him very well.

It was as cool in the gardens as he had predicted and Nancy shivered slightly as the night air wrapped round her. The music from the ballroom was muted and she watched for a moment as the dancers moved around the floor. Lights glowed on the path and tiny insects fluttered in the glare.

Suddenly she felt alone and a little afraid. It had been an adventurous step to come to Kenya by herself. Usually Richard's arm was there to guide her. He had always been the strong one who made decisions and she'd grown used to leaving everything to him. But Richard had gone from her life.

Although it was two months since they said goodbye, her heart still seemed frayed around the edges. It was hard to think of him without tears starting. For a moment she wondered if Richard would look at this same moon and think of her as she was thinking of him.

She sighed and turned towards the hotel. The door to the restaurant opened as some diners poured out, and she caught a glimpse of John sitting at the table where they had dined a few minutes earlier. Della Swan sat facing him, leaning forward, elbows on the table as she smiled, in rapt attention to their conversation. She wished she could see the expression on John Norris's face but his back was towards her and she was left to wonder. She looked at the ballroom again, then hesitantly retraced her steps along the path towards her room. It had been a long day. Thinking of Richard had stilled the excitement that bubbled in her heart but the wonder and magic of Kenya remained. Let's see what tomorrow brings, she thought as she quickened her footsteps.

2

The next morning, the persistent screeching and chattering of monkeys outside the bedroom window disturbed Nancy from a dreamless sleep. Stretching her arms, she yawned then, swinging her feet out of bed, padded across the room to draw back the curtains.

A startled monkey leaped from the balcony and on to the balustrade, baring its teeth in a vicious grimace as it eyed her from its precarious perch. Nancy chuckled, tapping a finger in a lively tattoo against the glass. The monkey scampered away, swinging to the branches of a nearby tree and was quickly lost from sight in the foliage.

Showering quickly, she wrapped a cotton skirt of rainbow colours around her bathing suit and shrugged into a cool blouse, tying it around her waist before venturing outside. The beach bag slung over one shoulder was heavy with the things she needed for the restful day planned by the pool, including a new novel she'd bought at the airport.

She ate breakfast alone at a secluded table by the door. There was no sight of John Norris, but as she was about to leave, Della Swan flounced into the restaurant with a sheaf of papers, closely followed by the young adminis-trator of the hotel.

She led the way to the table on the balcony and as she sat down she leaned towards John in an animated conversa-tion. As Nancy left, she was convinced that there was more than a working partnership between the two.

Picking her way across the lawns, Nancy wondered how many young women had been attracted to the personable John Norris. She assessed his attention of the previous evening as merely the consideration of an attentive hotel manager and surprised herself by feeling a slight pang of regret.

The morning by the pool passed in a haze of glorious sunshine, relieved by several refreshing, cool drinks. A breeze appeared unexpectedly some hours into the day, flapping the canopied umbrellas by the pool. A sudden gust blew Nancy's novel from her knee and sent it hurtling along the ground. She scrambled to her feet to retrieve it before it was swept into the pool but before she drew near enough, a man rose from a nearby sun lounger, picked up the book and walked towards her smiling as he waved it over his head.

'Obviously very light holiday reading,' he said with a grin. 'You should pick something more weighty next time. I would recommend 'War and Peace'. It would take a gale to blow that one away.'

Nancy thanked him.

'Actually, it's not quite as exciting as it looks on the cover. I'm rather bored with it,' she said shoving the paperback in her bag.

'Well, in that case perhaps you'd be glad of some company.'

He indicated a chair beside her. She smiled and nodded.

'Sit down, please.'

'I'm Kevin Moore. I'm only here for the day.'

He held out his hand and she bent forward to grasp it.

'Nancy Evans. I'm here for a fortnight.'

They laughed at their individual summaries.

'I'm intrigued.' Nancy frowned. 'How can you come to Mombasa's Diani Beach for a day? I thought everyone here was a package holidaymaker.'

'I'm a pilot on the tourist airline. I fly people up country to the safari game reserves. I have a flight tomorrow. It's an early start so I park myself here overnight.'

Nancy's eyes widened.

'How exciting! I was hoping to visit one of the reserves. It must be a wonderful experience.'

'You mustn't go home without seeing the animals in their natural surroundings. It will make your holiday, like the icing on the cake,' he said pointing a finger. 'Actually I've . . . '

At that moment, a smiling young Kenyan boy appeared at his elbow.

'Excuse me, missy, gentleman boss at café say you late.'

He pointed across the pool and Nancy saw the tall figure of John Norris beckoning her from the open-sided cafeteria. She stood up, apologising to Kevin who handed her the colourful skirt, slung over the back of his chair. She wrapped it around her waist and smiled, raising her shoulders.

'I'm sorry. I forgot about another arrangement. I'd love to hear more about the safaris if you're here later.'

'Oh, I'll still be here. I'll watch out for you,' he said, eyeing her appreciatively as she hurried away.

When she reached the cafeteria, John Norris frowned as she joined him at a table. He wagged a finger.

'Punctuality is the essence of good management,' he said sternly before his face relaxed into a grin. 'Did you forget our date?'

'I'm sorry.' Nancy nodded. 'I was so relaxed and warm and . . . '

'That's very pleasing to the management,' he broke in, 'but not very complimentary to me, seeing you forgot our lunch date. Anyway, you're here now.'

He slipped an arm casually around her shoulder and offered a chair.

'Unfortunately, I have a meeting of staff in an hour, so we must make the most of it. I have a little expedition arranged for five o'clock if you'd care to come along.'

Nancy beamed.

'Really? That's very kind of you. Where is it to . . . the expedition?'

'Well, we leave the hotel compound and walk along the road about a mile then cut through the plantation. There's a path of sorts, and we're going to visit a snake farm.'

31

Nancy's smile faded and she shivered slightly, leaning back in the chair.

'Oh,' she said pulling down the corners of her mouth. 'I hate snakes. They're awful creatures.'

John grinned.

'Oh, it's an opportunity not to be missed. You said you wanted to see local colour. Well, this is your first shot. Not going to chicken out, are you?'

'No.' Her voice was uncertain. 'I suppose it is safe and all that.'

'Just you wait and see. A memorable visit, I promise you.'

He grinned, ordering hamburgers and coffee with fruit salad to follow.

'Wasn't that Kevin Moore I saw you talking to?'

When she nodded he went on, 'I thought so. He has a party going to Amboseli Game Reserve tomorrow. By the way, what happened to you last night? I looked all over the grounds for you before going into the ballroom.'

Nancy was embarrassed, reluctant to mention that she had seen him in close conversation with Della Swan. The attractive girl had given Nancy all the signals that she was to keep away from the handsome administrator whom Della obviously had marked for herself.

'Well, it had been a long day so I turned in early. Sorry,' she added by way of an apology.

'Never mind, though I was disappointed not to find you.'

When the food arrived, they ate with relish and there was little opportunity for conversation until they pushed aside their plates.

'Nancy,' John began quietly, 'tell me to mind my own business if you wish but why are you alone?'

Before she had the chance to speak he went on.

'I was flicking through the bookings last night in the office and I noticed that there were two people originally booked in, then a cancellation.' He paused, looking at her intently. 'A boyfriend?'

Nancy nodded.

'We no longer see each other,' she said shortly and when he remained silent she felt compelled to explain. 'He had the opportunity to move, a promotion, you know the kind of thing. I didn't want to go. Simple as that.'

Richard had refused to listen to her argument, she recalled. He had been next in line for promotion at the marketing firm where he had worked since college. Its business was increasing rapidly and the prospects were far more promising than the job that had taken his eye up North. But the allurement of a company car and the pseudo title of Assistant Marketing Director had swayed his reasoning. When he stated bluntly, that if she didn't go with him they were finished, Nancy had taken him at his word.

She could still remember the look of surprise on his face when she walked out. It had taken all her inner reserves of strength but she knew she was right. Up to then Richard had always been right. He told her often enough and she'd been content to let him have his way in most things. But this time she looked to her own future. As private secretary to the director of a management consultant agency, she was content and settled in a job she liked and reluctant to move from her home town.

She was thankful she had at last seen the petty, spoiled little boy in him, angry because he could not manipulate her any longer. Yet, there were moments when all she could remember were the good times. As the disquieting memories flashed across her mind, Nancy realised that all she needed was a little more time to get her life on the right track again.

'So you came to Kenya alone to get over it,' John was saying as he patted her hand lying on the table then covered it with his own tanned fingers. 'Perhaps I'll be able to help you,' he said quietly.

'Isn't it time you were leaving for your meeting?' Nancy asked, relieved to be able to veer the conversation in another direction.

John Norris glanced at his watch and frowned.

'You're right. I've five minutes to get to the office. Walk with me.'

The path through the garden was fragrant with the scent of frangipani, white creamy blossoms that filled the air with their intoxicating aroma. Bending, he plucked a flower, holding it to his face before handing it to her.

'It's the colour of your skin,' he said smiling, 'but you'll see, before long this will be the shade of your tan.'

He pulled the blossom of a golden bougainvillaea and tossed it in the air, laughing as it circled before falling at their feet.

'Whatever you do, don't compete with the hibiscus.'

They were at the door into the hotel foyer, where he hesitated and pulled the head from one of the showy scarlet blossoms, tucking it behind her ear.

'Take care in the sun,' he said softly.

His face was only inches from her cheek and Nancy blushed, conscious of their closeness and felt herself stiffening in embarrassment.

'Boss, sir!'

One of the porters called urgently from the foyer and Norris sighed, smiling as he stepped away.

'Looks as if we're fated to be interrupted,' he said vaguely. 'Meet me at five o'clock sharp right here on the terrace. You won't forget now, will you? Five o'clock,' he called over his shoulder as he hurried away.

Turning towards the gardens, Nancy questioned why he was being so attentive, or was this the way he treated all his guests, she considered, hating herself for the recurrent twinge of regret.

When she arrived back at the pool, Kevin Moore lay glistening under a film of lotion. He had moved his sun lounger to lie next to hers and he looked up, shielding his eyes from the sun when she sat down to remove her skirt.

'You've been ages. I trust you haven't been eating all this time or you'll lose that shapely figure,' he teased.

Nancy hoped that the sun disguised her embarrassment as Kevin eyed her appraisingly through lowered eyelids. He stood up and reached for the bottle of sun lotion.

'Here, let me rub some cream on you. This is the hottest part of the day. Mustn't stay out in it too long unprotected.'

'No, really, I can manage.'

'No trouble at all,' he said bending over, 'just the opposite.'

He grinned as he sank on to the edge of the lounger and uncapped the bottle. Nancy turned over and felt the cool liquid drip on to her back then the slow movements of his strong fingers as they massaged her shoulders.

'I saw you were with John Norris. How I envy him his job here. He has the pick of all the ladies.' He laughed. 'That is when he can get out of Della's way. Incidentally, have you met our Della?'

His words were edged with sarcasm, and Nancy turned slightly to look at him, nodding.

'She makes a play for him at every opportunity, does Della. I think they used to be an item a while back, or that's what Della would have you believe. Don't know what soured it. I guess she's too damned possessive if you ask me and a bit too tied up with her own ego. There, that's better. Sorry there's not more of you. I quite enjoyed that.'

He grinned as he put the bottle to one side and wiped his hands on a towel. Nancy smiled, glancing at her watch.

'Must keep an eye on the time,' she said. 'I'll have to shower and change for five o'clock.'

Kevin threw back his head and laughed loudly.

'Oh, no, don't tell me you're going on the outing to the snake farm.'

'What's so funny about that?' she asked, instantly defensive and curious as she watched his shoulders heaving with hearty laughter.

'You'll see. I think I'll come along, for the experience. Five o'clock, eh?'

He chuckled as he stood up and made his way to the pool.

'I'm for a swim to cool off. Are you coming?'

Nancy watched as his tall lean figure teetered at the brink of the pool before diving in, cutting the water like a lance and disappearing beneath the ripples. He emerged some yards away and turned to wave. He was still laughing and Nancy's unease mounted, wondering why the mention of the snake farm had caused such amusement.

It was turned four o'clock when she collected her things and packed them into the bag.

'I'm going up to my room to get ready,' she said as she turned to leave.

Kevin stood up.

'Right, I'll see you over there at five then.'

Nancy felt easier by five o'clock when she stepped out of the lift into the hotel foyer as there were three young couples obviously waiting to go on the proposed outing. John Norris stood to one side in conversation with Kevin and they both smiled when Nancy joined them. But there was no sign of Della Swan and Nancy was instantly suspicious. Obviously Della knew from past experience what was afoot and Nancy's qualms increased.

Before she had time to ask any questions about the visit to the snake farm, two young Kenyan boys attracted their attention, waving the holidaymakers to follow. They both carried stout sticks that they circled in the air like batons.

'This way, please, ladies and gentlemen.'

The group followed in twos and threes, from the hotel compound on to the main road, walking along the grass verge to avoid the oncoming traffic. Crossing the road, John Norris took

Nancy's arm and smiled.

'You're looking very nervous. Nothing to worry about, really. Just stick with me. I'll look after you.'

Kevin followed, grinning widely as they crossed through the plantation.

'I'm surprised you bothered to come,' John said looking at him quizzically. 'You've been here before, haven't you?'

'Wouldn't miss this,' he said enigmatically, his grin widening.

The Kenyan guides led the way into a fenced enclosure, surrounded by overhanging trees and bushes that cut out any glimmer of sunlight. On all sides were wired cages with branches resting at an angle inside. One of the Kenyans raised his stick and rattled the wire mesh of the nearest cage, and a massive cobra raised its head from the coil that lay camouflaged by rotting leaves on the floor. It swayed from side to side puffing out its head and darting its forked tongue, angrily straining against the net.

The women shrieked in alarm and turned to grab their male companions who were also standing back at a safe distance, wide eyed, making feeble attempts to mask their own fear. Nancy felt John's arm close protectively around her and she leaned against him trembling, trying to overcome her very real terror of snakes. John's hand moved on her spine and the touch of his fingers was like electricity shooting through her body. She eased away from him, embarrassed by the contact.

The young man moved along the cages, rousing their occupants with his stick, sometimes opening the door to stir the snakes into movement. There were squeals and cries of alarm as the reptiles thrashed against the wire, furious to have been disturbed.

Cameras flashed as the tourists took their holiday snaps and some were brave enough to pose by the cages. Nancy felt John's arms tightening around her, his breath hot against her cheek and when she looked up at him in embarrassment he grinned.

'I told you it would be an enjoyable experience.'

His eyes sparkled as his fingers traced a path in the small of her back.

'I knew I'd enjoy it anyway,' he added.

She pushed him away, annoyed to have been so misled.

'I can see that,' she said sharply, edging away.

'Watch out!'

One of the Kenyan boys stepped back in alarm.

'The black mamba has escaped. Everyone stay where you are.'

Nancy held a hand to her mouth stifling the scream that rose harshly in her throat. A man's powerful arms closed around her and she willingly held on, burying her face in his chest. His cool lips brushed her cheek.

'It's only a joke, don't worry.'

A firm hand smoothed her hair and when she looked up it was Kevin Moore who held her, pulling her so tightly to him that she could hear the thud of his heartbeat. She glanced over his shoulder and met the hostile eyes of John Norris glaring beneath a frown that contorted his face.

3

The party reassembled for the trek back to the Hotel Africana, bubbling with high spirits and chuckling at the practical joke. Some disclosed that they had been given a suggestion of what was to come by the two Kenyans on the way there.

'The men will enjoy the visit most,' they had said, winking broadly. 'Every time we come to snake farm, the men go away smiling.'

Nancy clenched her teeth, remembering Kevin's amusement and him saying he would come along for the experience. She seethed with annoyance. The visit was obviously set up to send the frightened women running into the arms of the nearest man. And he had made sure he was nearest. No wonder John looked riled.

She saw the humour but felt annoyed

to have been their target, feeling bruised and vulnerable. The possibility that she'd looked foolish made her cringe. Glancing over her shoulder she noticed Kevin and John lagged behind the rest. Kevin winked, a huge smile erupting from his craggy face. John's head was bent low and he intently watched every step, picking his way along the narrow path, grim and unsmiling.

At the hotel, Nancy crossed the foyer, waiting for the lift. Listening to the excited chatter of the others making arrangements to meet later, an intense sensation of loneliness wrapped round her. For a moment, she felt again the comfort of Richard's arm but he was no longer there . . . would never be there again. She willed the lift to appear.

Kevin came in followed by John who stood for a moment looking at her, hands thrust in pockets. A frown crossed his face and he turned away abruptly, seeing Kevin cross the foyer towards her.

'A long cool drink?' he invited.

Nancy forced a smile through the clutter of emotions. The memory of having clung to him so tightly still lingered and she blushed.

'I'm going to have a quiet read before dinner.'

'Oh, please,' he pleaded like a persistent child. 'I'm not dining here tonight. I have to go to the air strip to make instrument checks and such. Then I'll be turning in. Up at the crack of dawn,' he added. 'So one drink,' he urged, 'to wish me a safe journey?'

The smile starting in his eyes, crept over his face and Nancy knew it would have been churlish to refuse. She shrugged.

'One drink.'

They walked across the lawns to the bar. Kevin grinned, glancing out of the corner of his eye.

'Enjoy the snake farm?'

She glared but, totally disarmed by his look of abject innocence, gave way to a smile.

'Least said, the better. No wonder you were amused when I mentioned it earlier.'

'I told you it would be a memorable experience. There'll be a greater thrill in store if you join one of the safaris. I'm going up country again at the weekend. You said you wanted to go to the reserve. Why don't you book a place with Della?'

Nancy flopped on to a chair.

'That would be great. I'll see her and make arrangements.'

He leaned across the table peering into her face and for a moment there was only inches between them. Nancy sat back and smiled. She attached no importance to his flirtatious manner knowing that, like the visit to the snake farm, he had said and done it all before. But she had to admit, Kevin was just the company needed to blow away the cobwebs.

As if reading her thoughts he said quietly, 'I don't do this with every young lady who throws herself at me in terror.'

He chuckled, his eyes wide and innocent. Nancy laughed at his innocent expression.

'Now, a cocktail. It has to be the Safari Adventure in the circumstances.'

Kevin went to the bar, lolling against the counter, chatting amicably to the beaming attendant. Nancy tingled with excitement. Only her second day in Kenya and she had attracted the attention of the two most handsome men she had seen in the hotel. It was boosting her ego beyond recall, and though she realised the fine words were lighthearted and flippant, it was all a pleasant antidote to her depression.

She glanced out to the terrace. John Norris was looking at the bar and, when his eyes lighted on Kevin, he frowned, pushed both hands into his pockets and went inside. Kevin, blissfully unaware he was under scrutiny, walked carefully across the grass holding two tall glasses filled to the brim with pale green liquid. Slices of orange and lemon were curved on to the sugared rim and a cardboard lion resplendent with a curly paper mane towered from the top.

'Two Safari Adventures,' he said, setting the glasses down. 'Cheers!'

Her eyes were wide and shining as her fingers closed around the tumbler to return the toast. Kevin grinned as he drained his glass.

'Here's to the weekend. You'll have a great time, I promise you. And now, sweet lady with bright eyes, I'll have to be on my way to the airstrip.'

As they walked back into the foyer, Kevin's responses to Nancy's questions about the game reserve lifted her spirits no end. When they reached the lift, she remembered how downhearted she had been earlier standing in the same spot and a feeling of relief coloured her thoughts as she turned to smile. He moved closer, taking her hand.

'Don't let any scheming hotel managers sidetrack you while I'm away,' he said in a low, conspiratorial voice.

'I'm not very popular in that quarter at the moment. He seems offended.'

'He'll bounce back, you'll see.'

The lift arrived and Nancy stepped in.

'Goodbye, have a safe journey.'

Kevin planted a swift kiss on her cheek.

' 'Bye, see you in a couple of days.'

As the door slid shut, Nancy held a hand to her face, chuckling. Kevin was undoubtedly a smoothie but he was so charming it was impossible to take offence at his outrageous actions.

The refreshing cool of the air conditioning swirled over Nancy as soon as she opened her bedroom door. On the dressing table a vase of freshly-picked frangipani blossoms tumbled on to the polished wood. Nancy buried her face in the waxy petals. There was no card and she wondered if it was hotel policy to provide flowers for the guests.

Shedding her clothes, she lay down on the bed. Closing her eyes, sleep came quickly.

She awoke to find the room in near

darkness. Switching on the bedside lamp to glance at her watch, Nancy groaned . . . nine o'clock! Hurrying into the bathroom, she drew a hand through tangled hair. After a hasty shower, she selected a white dress with a full skirt. It was comfortably cool, accentuating the beginnings of a tan. She turned to the door, wincing as hunger pangs gnawed. She hesitated, selecting a single frangipani flower and pinned it to her dress.

The air was stifling as she hurried to the restaurant. The maître d'hôtel greeted her with a friendly smile, sweeping the door aside in a courtly gesture. He led the way to the table on the balcony where John Norris sat, head down, tracing patterns on the tablecloth with a fingertip. He stood up and smiled as she walked towards him.

'I was about to send a message to your room to see if you were all right.'

'I'm afraid I fell asleep.'

'Then the rest has done you good. You look wonderful,' he said, his eyes warming in an appreciative smile. 'You liked my flowers?'

He nodded to the frangipani. She nodded back, feeling the colour rush to her cheeks.

'About this afternoon . . . '

'Forget it,' she said. 'I have.'

'The snake farm is arranged for the guests,' he began hesitantly. 'It's an experience people enjoy, take photos . . . that sort of thing. And the joke about the escaped snake usually gives everyone a good laugh. I'm sorry I laid you open to it.'

'I was embarrassed when I realised I had jumped into Kevin's arms.'

'And I was too far away at the time,' he said, grinning.

Their laughter broke down the barrier that lay between them and when the meal arrived, John tucked in swiftly. Nancy set about her meal with the same zeal, taking an interest in all the dishes set before them. When they finished, each sat back and sighed with satisfaction.

'Let's walk through the garden for a breather then have a drink at the bar,' John suggested.

Outside, he took her hand, tucking it into the crook of his arm.

'Hello, there!'

Della Swan hurried towards them, her eyes narrowing, resting briefly on Nancy's hand held firmly in John's.

'There's someone at reception looking for you, Miss Evans. Some good news. I'll let him tell you.'

Her regulation smile appeared briefly, disappearing as rapidly when John took charge.

'Let's see what this is about.'

An ebony-faced policeman chatted to the reception clerk, flashing a flawless smile.

'Miss Nancy Evans? I have recovered your flight bag.'

'Oh, that's wonderful, thank you.'

Nancy reached for it, smiling at John who was questioning the officer.

'Is everything there?'

'Miss Evans' passport is safe, also her

flight ticket. The only thing missing is the English money. The thief will not be able to exchange it. We have strict regulations about the barter of foreign currency.'

He beamed at Nancy.

'Have you caught the boy who snatched the bag?' John said.

'Yes. He is twelve years old. We will see that he is punished.'

Nancy toyed with the strap of the flight bag as she checked the contents.

'I've got it back. Let the matter rest. I don't want to get the child into any more trouble. Can't you let him off with a stern warning?'

'I'm sure they will do what is right,' John said and took the bag from Nancy's hand, giving it to the clerk. 'See this is taken to Miss Evans' room.'

They left the policeman and headed back to the terrace.

'We have to celebrate the return of the missing bag. Let's go before there are more interruptions.'

Sauntering through the gardens Nancy

said quietly, 'I thought my holiday was doomed from the start but it seems everything's falling nicely into place. It's turning out to be much better than I expected.'

'I'm glad, Nancy, and this is just the beginning.'

'Kevin suggested I should book a seat on the safari group to Amboseli at the weekend. I'm so excited at the prospect. It sounds wonderful.'

John patted her hand and smiled at her eager expression.

'I wish I could share that glorious moment when you see your first herd of elephants. It's a sight you'll never forget. Come on, let's walk on the beach. You can slip off your shoes.'

Nancy did as he suggested when they reached the sand, sifting it through her toes like powder. She shivered.

'I should have brought a cardigan.'

He untangled his arm from hers, draping it around her shoulders.

'Let me keep you warm,' he said with a slow smile.

She felt the warmth of his body as he held her closely and the tang of musky aftershave blended with the blossom pinned to her dress, filling the air with a medley of scents. She knew he was going to kiss her when he suddenly stopped and her body tensed.

'Nancy,' he whispered, pulling her towards him. 'You're cold.'

His arms closed around her and blood raced as she felt the heat of his breath on her cheek. Suddenly his lips were cool against her mouth. She stiffened and his reaction was immediate. He stepped away, taking her hand.

'We'd better go in.'

His face was lined with suppressed tension and Nancy trembled at the passion that lay there. He drew a finger gently over her cheek.

'I'm going to dance with you all night long. At least I'll have an excuse to hold you in my arms.'

She smiled, hoping the moonlight left her face in shadows. The blush was as disquieting as the trembling of butterfly wings that had invaded her stomach, telling her that things were moving much too fast.

They sat in a quiet corner of the bar, ordering drinks from the grinning attendant who bowed as he advanced on their table.

'Yes, Mister Norris boss?'

'That's Daniel,' he explained. 'His father works here in the gardens and his elder brother is one of the porters.'

'You know all their names?' Nancy asked in astonishment.

'I try to.'

'And the guests?' Nancy said quietly. 'Do you plan your action before they arrive and select the unaccompanied females for special attention?'

She knew the words sounded bitter but the memory of his kiss on the beach was too recent and although she was lonely, she neither wanted nor needed a romantic interlude. Glancing at him, Nancy tried to ignore the attraction that caused her heart to pound more rapidly.

'No, I don't. Neither do I hand out pens at the reception desk on a regular basis,' he replied.

'Well, looks like I was the lucky one.'

Nancy tried to pass off her remark by laughing lightly.

'No, Nancy. I'm the lucky one. It's me you're sitting with right now and it was me who had the joy of kissing you a minute ago on the beach.'

He moved closer and rested an arm on the back of her chair.

'I'm glad your boyfriend cancelled the trip or I might never have got the chance to do this.'

He leaned forward and kissed her again, cupping her head in his palm, just as Daniel arrived with the drinks. She bent forward to pick up her drink but his hand was there first. He gave her the cold glass and held up his, chinking the glasses.

'To you and me. This is the beginning of . . . '

'Of what?'

The words came out more curtly

than Nancy had intended but John merely shook his head and smiled into her eyes.

'Of something special, Nancy. I knew it the moment I saw you. All I know is that something hit me here.'

He thumped his chest, and she grinned and raised her shoulders.

'Indigestion! It has to be the cream of coconut soup. Very rich, I hear.'

Their laughter lightened the tension but later, when John stood up and reached for her, she felt again the strength of his arms closing around her as they swayed to the music on the crowded dance floor. His mouth lingered on her ear and the hot breath filled her with an excitement she tried to still.

This was too sudden her heart pounded. How could she allow herself to be attracted to anyone so soon after the pain of Richard? She would be home in two weeks and never see John again. There could be no more heartache. She must end this before it began.

Much later, Nancy glanced at her watch and her eyes widened.

'It's two o'clock!'

John nodded as they left the floor to sit at their table in the corner.

'You haven't seen an African dawn yet. It's the most spectacular sight you'll ever see.'

'But that's hours away yet. It sounds wonderful but . . . '

'Stay with me. Let me show you Kenya in all its glory. I want . . . '

He leaned forward and kissed her cheek, grasping her trembling fingers in a tight fist. Oblivious of the remaining dancers and the bar attendants who padded around clearing the deserted tables, he pulled her into his arms and held her closely.

'John,' she whispered, pushing him away gently. 'It's very late and I'm tired. I really must go.'

He nodded and sighed deeply.

'I'll take you to your room.'

They walked slowly through the gardens and into the foyer. When the lift arrived she turned to look at him shyly.

'Well, thank you . . . '

'I'll see you to your door,' he insisted.

Outside, she fumbled for her key and he took it from her, turning it in the lock and pushing the door open. He stood aside and reached for her hands, raising them to his lips.

'The pool cafeteria, one o'clock sharp,' he said simply, as with a determined effort, he gently moved away. 'Remember.'

'I'll remember.'

On impulse, she stood on her toes and kissed him lightly on the cheek before going inside and closing the door. Leaning against the sturdy frame, she fought to control the rapid breaths that tore from her chest, leaving her weak and unresolved.

Nancy sank on to the edge of the bed, trying to analyse her feelings. Because of John, she had barely thought of Richard all night and a pang of guilt tore at her heart until she remembered, there was no reason to feel that she had betrayed Richard by being attracted to another man. She was a free agent these days, wasn't she?

She sighed, suddenly so tired with all the emotion that had been directed at her tonight. She undressed swiftly and tumbled into bed, drawing the cool sheet up to her chin. Blissfully comfortable, the events of the day, coupled with the afterglow of the sunshine, lulled her into a calmer frame of mind and swiftly, she drifted into sleep . . .

Nancy was among the last holiday-makers to enter the dining-room the next morning and as she selected scrambled eggs and fruit juice from the buffet she became aware of a buzz of animated conversation at one of the tables. Della Swan, draining her coffee cup, looked up and caught her eye, nodding briskly before gathering a sheaf of papers from the table. She assembled them into a pile and was preparing to leave when an agitated woman approached.

'Is it true?' she asked in a loud voice. 'Has that nice young pilot really had an accident?'

Della nodded, pursing her lips.

'Don't worry. Everything's OK. Your safari trip's still on for the end of the week. We'll arrange another plane if necessary.'

'Oh! That's all right then.'

The woman walked off, waving at Della as she left the dining-room.

As Della passed, Nancy called, 'Has Kevin had an accident?'

The courier paused, nodding.

'The passengers are all right. It happened after he dropped them at the reserve, on his way to refuel. Something to do with the landing mechanism.'

Her lips curved in a thin smile as she passed out of the room. Nancy sat down, shuddering at the news, wondering if Kevin really was all right.

4

Nancy stretched on the sunlounger and picked up the paperback, flicking the pages absentmindedly as her mind raced with concern that Kevin might be badly injured. In the end she laid the book aside and closed her eyes. She was anxious to have accurate news.

Nearing one o'clock, she slipped on her sandals and padded around the pool to the cafeteria to wait for John, hoping he'd have the latest report on the accident. When he hadn't arrived by twenty past one, she ordered a sandwich, and returned to the sunlounger.

Some time later, a hotel porter approached and bowed from the waist. Nancy looked up and smiled. The young man handed her a letter and waited whilst Nancy ripped open the envelope.

Dear Nancy,
Sorry I couldn't make it for lunch.
I'll explain at dinner — seven sharp.
John.

Nancy picked up her novel but the words blurred and her mind wandered aimlessly all afternoon. Gathering her belongings, she eventually made for her room, planning a long, cool shower before dressing for dinner.

Nancy took time at the mirror to arrange her hair, secured with tiny diamante clips at each side. Pinning a matching brooch on her black sheath dress, she was ready. John was already at the table when she went down.

'Nancy!'

His eyes, glowing with an appreciative smile, slowly washed over her appraisingly. Nancy felt the familiar tremor start in her throat.

'I'm sorry about lunch. I got a message to you as soon as I could.'

'I grabbed a sandwich. When it got to twenty past one I knew Mr Punctuality

Norris must have had a more promising offer,' she said, smiling.

'Oh, no!' he hastened to explain. 'One of my staff was rushed into hospital. An accident with some machinery. More of a fright than anything else.'

'It's been a day for accidents,' Nancy said. 'Kevin . . . '

'He's OK. Della told me as I left for the hospital. Nothing seriously damaged, only his pride and the aircraft. That'll put him out of action on both fronts for a while.'

'Sounds as if you don't like Kevin very much.'

'He's all right. Not keen on his type.'

'What does that mean? He seemed charming, what I saw of him.'

'No doubt he'll be charming the nurses by now.'

The cryptic remark left Nancy puzzled.

She eyed John across the table as he studied the menu, trying to understand why he had rushed to the bedside of his employee, yet failed to show compassion for Kevin who could have been killed when his plane crashed. The man, and his attitudes, were a mystery.

As they were finishing their meal, John groaned. His eyes narrowed as the trim figure of Della purposefully advanced in their direction.

'So sorry to interrupt but I thought you'd like to know Kevin's been discharged from hospital and he's coming to the coast for a couple of days' rest. He should be back in action for the weekend. I'm so pleased. There's been so many grumbles about cancelled safaris. Can I interest you in a flight?' she said turning to Nancy. 'I'll leave a leaflet.'

She laid a brochure by Nancy's plate and left, threading her way through the holidaymakers delivering her good news. John turned back to his dessert and they finished dinner without speaking.

'Now, a brisk walk on the beach is recommended by the management.'

John pushed back his chair. Nancy remembered the heat of his passion and frenzied kisses the last time they walked on the sands. Would she halt his advances should he do the same again?

'He was lucky, Kevin,' she said as they walked from the restaurant. 'To have got off so lightly. He could have been seriously hurt, even killed.'

They'd reached the steps leading to the beach. John stopped and faced her.

'Don't waste too much sympathy on Kevin. He's a reckless sort of guy, with women and planes. Don't let him get under your skin.'

'I've got my feet firmly on the ground. I won't let my emotions run away with me . . . ever again . . . with Kevin or anyone else.'

Biting her lip, she turned and began to walk away but his powerful arms halted her. Spinning her round to face him, his mouth closed on her parted lips. When he released her, Nancy was alarmed at the ferocity in his voice.

'Nancy, I'm in love with you.'

The anger halted in her throat and she swallowed with difficulty, not believing the words he repeated, more gently this time.

'I'm in love with you. I'm not Kevin passing away the hours or your boyfriend hurting you. I want to take the pain away and make you happy. Give me a chance, Nancy, please.'

'I don't understand. We don't even know each other. It's too sudden.'

'I see such a hurt look in your eyes, Nancy. I want to take it away. I know I can if you give me a chance.'

Nancy felt tears behind her eyes and she looked away.

'Don't you dare feel sorry for me, John Norris. I can make my own decisions. I was the one who walked away from Richard. He wanted to pin me down. I think I had a happy escape. We'd have had a pretty dull life, Richard and I. Maybe he was right. Perhaps I will be a provincial mouse all my life but I'll make my own decisions.'

In a second, his arms were round her

holding her closely and the gentle comforting stroke of his fingers on her hair unleashed a torrent of tears.

Nancy realised she had never before let anyone see her tears. Maybe the pain was all in the past, and she was finding herself again. Now she could plan for her future, a future where Richard no longer had a part. It was as if the tears had washed away the heartache.

'I'm sorry,' she whispered. 'I'm embarrassed that you've seen all this.'

John reached in his pocket for a handkerchief and tenderly wiped her face, kissing each cheek in turn.

'Better now?'

She nodded.

'Then let's walk.'

There was an almost tangible calmness between them as they ambled along the beach.

'Nancy,' he said quietly, his hand tightening, 'come and live in Kenya.'

She gasped, stopping to look at him.

'That's a big step for a provincial mouse.'

'Come to Kericho with me. That's what I've always wanted to do. Live on the hillsides near the Rift Valley where the scenery's so unbelievable it takes your breath away. The climate's so comfortable, almost like home.'

'Are you thinking of moving to another hotel?'

'No . . . no hotel, no residents grumbling because their soup's lukewarm or because they've got cuts and grazes round the pool. Peace and quiet for me and as much tea as you can drink.'

He chuckled at her puzzled expression.

'That's where we grow tea. My father has interests in a plantation there. He turned to that when he left the diplomatic service. Whenever I visit them I hate to leave. It's a different world. A world of real people, not this false ambience put on for tourists out to let their hair down on holiday.'

Nancy sighed.

'It's so beautiful here. I'm surprised

you've even considered moving.'

'It's always been at the back of my mind but it's only since I met you that I've thought about it in earnest.'

Nancy shook her head.

'Oh, John! How can you expect me to take such a proposal to heart? I've only been here a couple of days and you're suggesting I throw discretion to the winds and start a new life in a strange country with a man I've only just met. How can I possibly take you seriously.'

She stepped away, pulling herself free of his arm.

'Nancy,' he said softly, facing her squarely, 'how long did you know Richard?'

The unexpected question unbalanced her.

'About three years,' she stammered. 'Why do you ask me that?'

'You thought that you knew him, yet it took all that time to find out the truth. It proves that time doesn't really count for that much. Three days is enough for me . . . for you, too, if . . . '

'He only wanted me to go three hundred miles away. You're expecting me to move to a different world. John we're strangers.'

'No!'

He moved towards her and held her shoulders, shaking her gently.

'There's a magnetism between us, Nancy. You feel it and so do I. You can't deny it. Fall in love with Kenya, maybe then I'll have a chance, too.'

There was a weakness in her knees and Nancy leaned against him, fearing she would fall. This was all happening too fast. How could she take him seriously? How many others had he said this to before?

As his lips met hers, consuming her in a kiss that took her breath away, Nancy no longer cared. This was a moment to be savoured. Suddenly, she shivered.

'You're cold?'

John draped his arm around her shoulders.

'We'll go back inside. There's lots

more to say but we have plenty of time ahead of us, Nancy. How much depends on you.'

Inside, they danced until it was late.

Before returning to the reception area, John hesitated and bent to kiss her trembling lips. A voice from behind them made them jump apart.

'Mr Norris, boss. Please, sir. Need to see you most urgently. Trouble with air-conditioning.'

Nancy smiled as John ran an impatient hand through his hair and turned to look at her with a quizzical expression.

'I'll see you tomorrow, John. It looks like you're needed.'

She stood on tiptoe and kissed him lightly on the cheek then turned away towards the lift.

'Till tomorrow,' he said softly, the words filled with promise.

5

Della Swan was holding an impromptu meeting with her clients by the pool. A cluster of holidaymakers gathered around as she waved a clip board. Eventually the group dispersed with a volley of noisy repartee and Della turned away to collect her belongings.

Watching from where she lay on a lounger, Nancy envied the courier's confidence as Della walked towards her.

'Hi!'

She pulled a chair into the shade of the umbrella and Nancy wondered why Della was displaying such friendliness.

'I'm going for a long, cold shower now then stretching out on the bed.'

She raised a manicured hand to her mouth hiding the yawn that temporarily distorted her face.

'John and I were up until daybreak

trying to sort out the air conditioning. I had fifteen complaints last night from clients. But John had everything under control. He's a marvel with the staff, so capable.'

She sighed, suggesting deep thoughts by her expression.

'He gets the very best out of them and that's not always easy.'

'So what time did you eventually get it fixed?' Nancy inquired.

'Must have been four-thirty. By then we were so hot, we went for a leisurely dip in the pool by moonlight. So refreshing. I was all in but John can be so persuasive.'

She sighed, closing her eyes as if revelling in the memory. Nancy's cheeks burned.

'No wonder you're tired,' she said, veiling the tightness of her voice with a veneer of friendliness.

'Anyway, enough about John and me. What about . . . '

Nancy's heart lurched. The words slipped so easily from her tongue, John and me! Kevin had said they were an item at one time. She began to wonder, was it over? John criticised Kevin for his easy show of charm. Perhaps he had a familiar line of his own. With a start, she heard Della repeating a question.

'What about the safari trip to Amboseli Game Reserve? I gave you a leaflet last night at dinner. Have you given it any thought? I'm taking bookings and the aircraft's almost full.'

Their conversation was interrupted by a woman who hovered at Della's side. After the exchange of a few words Della stood, shrugging.

'I'm going to be busy for a while. See you later. Let me know about the trip,' she called over her shoulder.

Nancy was plagued by the gnawing doubts of her heart. I'm making a fool of myself, she thought. I was right. John has his pick of the guests. No wonder he waits at the reception desk. That way he sees the unaccompanied females arrive. In spite of the sun being at its highest, Nancy shivered with anger and frustration.

Stomping to the pool, she plunged into its blue depths, cutting the surface like a spear. The water closed overhead, soft and silky against her skin and she revelled in the coolness.

Surfacing in the centre, she saw John making for the cafeteria. Remembering the usual arrangement to meet for lunch, she trod water indecisively. She wanted to avoid him, fearing that should they meet, her words of reproach would flood unchecked. Her doubts regarding the sincerity of his affections were now justified by what she had heard from Della. She was dismayed at her lack of commonsense. How could she have been such a fool to believe him?

John glanced around, pushing his hands into his pockets, the frown deepening. He looked at his watch then began to walk slowly back to the hotel terrace. Satisfied he was gone, Nancy slid out of the pool. Hastily drying herself, she gathered her belongings and made for the sunbeds on the lawns. She selected one in the shade.

How many times, she wondered, had John tried that polished line about staying in Kenya with other solitary, women guests? And how many conquests had he made by the empty words? She resolved that from now on she would avoid him. If they met by chance in the hotel, she would treat him with restraint. From now on her feet were on firm ground.

A familiar figure strode towards her. Kevin Moore hurried across the grass. In a couple of strides he was beside her.

'Kevin! How are you?'

Nancy laughed as he pirouetted on the lawn to the amusement of those nearby.

'Look, not a scratch, not even a bruise . . . well, none that show anyway.'

He flopped on the ground, cradling his knees.

'Well, have you waited for me, Nancy?'

She ignored the question, saying, 'You were lucky to have got off so lightly. You could have been killed.'

'Only the good die young. I'm going to be around a long time yet. Hey! Do you fancy a ride to the shopping precinct? It's not much, but there's a selection of souvenirs . . . the usual things laid on for tourists.'

Nancy sat up, perching on the end of the lounger.

'Sounds great. Give me ten minutes,' she said and ran indoors.

He was waiting by the lift when she re-appeared and propelled her towards the low sports car parked in the drive. Kevin drove in the direction of the main road and Nancy delighted in the warm current of air flowing on her face and hair.

A cluster of flat white buildings loomed in the distance, a few miles along the road. Kevin pulled into a parking area. Threading in and out of the tiny supermarket was an incongruous smattering of tourists, mingling with locals dressed in their colourful costumes.

He led her along the paved area to a tiny café busy with tourists. They selected a table in the shade and ordered cool drinks. Nancy watched as people emerged from the busy super-market with their plastic carrier bags.

'Don't think it's like this for everyone,' Kevin commented. 'There's poverty here that surpasses your imagination. These are the lucky ones. Away from the tourist areas people scratch out a living where they can. Luckily tourism is spreading into the bush because of the Game Reserves so more workers are needed. It all helps.'

'So you do approve of us?'

'I approve of you, Nancy. No wonder Norris picked you out.'

She flinched.

'Does he make a habit of selecting his targets at Reception? I suppose I'm only one of a line.'

Nancy found it hard to disguise the bitterness as her fists closed into a tight ball in her lap. She saw Kevin grin.

'Can't say I'd blame him if he did,' he said lightly, not taking the question as seriously as Nancy intended. 'He got tangled with Della a while back and he plays safe these days. Della's quite a girl. She's ambitious. She'd take over the hotel if John let her. Anyway, what's this interest in Norris? Has he been casting his net?'

'My head's not easily turned, I assure you, and if he has been casting the net, then I haven't been caught,' she said slowly with some embarrassment.

Nancy no longer wished to pursue the character of John Norris and she veered the conversation away.

'I've been thinking about the trip to the Amboseli Game Reserve. Della gave me a leaflet. I'm going to put my name on the list,' she said quietly.

'You'll have a great time. I'll escort you myself,' Kevin said with a mischievous wink which instantly raised her spirits.

He pushed back his chair and led her across the tiny square to a small gift shop which they browsed through briefly. The air was stifling. Kevin mopped his brow as they went outside.

'Shall we go back to the hotel and jump in the pool?'

Nancy nodded. Back at the Hotel Africana, she saw John surrounded by a group of porters, giving them a list of orders in effortless Swahili. Catching sight of them he paused for a moment and as Nancy crossed to the lift, she knew his eyes were following her.

'I'll see you at the pool in five minutes,' she said to Kevin taking care to avoid looking in John's direction.

He was waiting on the terrace when she came down, however, brows drawn together and his mouth sealed in a tight line.

'I wondered what happened to you at the cafeteria but now I know,' he said sternly, glancing across the lawns. 'I see you had a better diversion.'

'It wasn't like that,' she stammered. 'Anyway, according to Della, you were both enjoying a romantic swim by moonlight as a prelude to the remainder of the night. I merely thought your breakfast would have clashed with our lunch.'

His face relaxed into a smile.

'I see,' he said shortly. 'Actually, we had a long and tiresome search for an air vent fault that was bringing in complaints by the minute. I gave instructions that if a complaint was received from your room I would attend to that in person.'

The disarming grin threw Nancy off course and she hung her head, reluctant to meet his eyes.

'There were four of the staff engineers apart from myself and Della. Incidentally, she was more of a hindrance than a help. After we'd located the fault we all had a swim to cool off before we retired for what was left of the night. That's all there was to it.'

Nancy coloured under the glow of her tan. Della's mischievous insinuations had been intended to arouse the very feelings Nancy had been only too ready to display. She felt mean and suspicious, relieved when he passed over the subject and asked, 'Where have you been?'

'Kevin took me to the shopping area, and I'm booking a seat on the outing to the game reserve. I'm looking forward to it. I'm meeting him at the pool to cool off, so if you'll excuse me, I don't want to keep him waiting.'

His mouth closed into a tight line and he flexed his shoulders, making a noticeable effort to speak calmly.

'Enjoy your swim,' he said coldly. 'However, I shall be waiting for you at dinner as usual. You do have to eat,' he added with a sardonic smile.

She dressed carefully for dinner that evening choosing a cool, cotton skirt in a delicate shade of blue with a matching chemise trimmed with marguerites. John was in the restaurant when she arrived. They spoke little throughout the meal. Nancy was aware of John's magnetism when their eyes met by chance. She couldn't deny the thrill of excitement that sent shivers up and down her spine.

Silently, she reproached herself. Now she must face the battle of reassessing her feelings again. He had cured her of thinking about Richard but now the cure was proving to be more devastating than the malady.

After they had eaten John asked, 'Have you packed for Amboseli?'

She shook her head.

'Five minutes will do.' She laughed. 'I won't need much for two days.'

'It's very dusty in the game parks and it can be sticky in the heat of midday. You'll need plenty of creams for your skin, shorts, T-shirts and . . . '

'And a little black number for the evenings,' she added, grinning. 'You sound like an expert from a fashion magazine.'

There was a hint of sarcasm in her words but if he recognised it, he failed to respond. Instead he smiled, wiping his mouth with the napkin.

'By the way, I've arranged another

seat on the plane. I'm taking some days off,' he said casually. 'You can't escape me as easily as you thought.'

Nancy was at a loss for words. Her heart pounded as she stared at him.

'Nancy . . . '

She cringed from whatever else he had to say, feeling like an animal caught in the headlights of a passing car. With thoughts of her own survival she shrugged.

'We hardly know each other. What do you want from me, John?'

Her words trailed as she pleaded, hardly recognising the tone of her voice, faltering and trembling with disbelief.

John clamped his lips together in a straight line. A nerve twitched at the corner of his mouth as his jaw tightened. He smiled and caressed her hand with gentle strokes.

'I want you with me, Nancy. When your holiday's over I want you to stay on in Kenya and we'll move to the plantation in Kericho as soon as I can arrange it. Stay with me, Nancy. I do love you,' he said quietly.

If only she could believe him, her heart cried. But how could he love her? She couldn't allow herself to make the same mistake as she'd made with Richard. He, too, had declared his love, yet he had been willing to leave her behind. John, too, would turn away if another more attractive holidaymaker came on the scene. And then there was Della Swan. Where did she fit in?

Nancy gave herself a shake as she looked at him across the table. His eyes bore into hers with their intensity as he lifted her trembling hand to his mouth and planted small kisses on each finger in turn. The moment passed and Nancy was relieved that he had not pressed for an answer for she realised the truth was there was nothing she wanted more than to stay with him. But the fear of being hurt again prevented her from making any rash promises she would live to regret.

6

Nancy barely slept thinking of the trip to Amboseli. After a hasty shower she dressed quickly in light cotton slacks and a scarlet T-shirt, throwing a chunky sweater into her bag. Grabbing the holdall, she hurried downstairs for breakfast, doubting that she would eat because of the excitement.

John was chatting to Kevin and Della. Even at this time of the morning, Nancy thought with a touch of envy, Della looks as if she's stepped out of a fashion plate picture from a magazine. They greeted Nancy, and John led her to the table on the balcony.

'I'll bring you something.'

He returned balancing a tray with cereal, scrambled egg, toast and fruit juice, setting it down with an encouraging smile.

'All intrepid white hunters must eat a

hearty breakfast.'

Nancy was relieved when it was time to leave. The sun was now risen, and already the temperature soared. The heat was rising from the pavement as they walked to the car which would take them to the first air strip.

Della stayed behind to usher her party into a minibus, ticking names on her list as Kevin got into the back of the car with Nancy. John climbed in beside the driver, who started up the engine and set off.

Kevin squeezed Nancy's hand.

'You have a great experience ahead of you. This will make your visit to Kenya worthwhile.'

Nancy smiled and caught a glimpse of John staring at her in the mirror, his face devoid of expression. The hotel was soon behind them as they drove along the highway overtaking early-morning traffic. Turning off the main road, the car bumped along a rutted track to a clearing where a solitary hangar gleamed in the morning sunshine. Kevin disappeared inside. After a few moments a tiny aeroplane taxied into view and stopped in front of the waiting area.

'It's so small,' Nancy commented.

'It's quite safe.' John grinned. 'Let's get on board before Della brings her gang. You'll enjoy it. It's like riding the Big Dipper.'

His eyes glinted mischievously noting her apprehension. Nancy followed, fearful at the thought of flying in the tiny aircraft. Kevin threw their bags into the tail section and Nancy settled, strapping the belt firmly before looking out of the window.

The minibus with Della and her passengers was drawing to a halt near the plane and the excited holidaymakers piled out. Soon everyone was aboard and Della completed her checks. She sidled up the aisle to Kevin then made her way to Nancy.

'Kevin refuses to take off until you sit up front,' she said with a grin, leaning past John to release Nancy's seat belt.

As Nancy took up her new seat, she

glanced back in time to see Della's smug smile as she snuggled closer to John, draping herself over his arm. John was impassive, gazing out of the window.

The plane taxied along the runaway then turned. Kevin adjusted his headgear and muttered into the radio, then, gathering speed, the plane lifted off the ground and circled the tiny air strip before banking inland. Nancy clamped her lips together, trying to ignore the lurch. As the plane soared high into the sky, the airpockets were less noticeable and she relaxed, watching the greenness of the countryside slip farther away.

Nearing the end of their journey, Kevin nudged her, saying, 'Look, Nancy, Mount Killimanjaro.'

The sprawling mountain was crowned with a trailing cloud that obligingly drifted away even as they looked. The snow-capped peak seemed to thrust into space. Nancy's eyes widened as she gazed on the sight that had thrilled travellers for centuries.

'Look!' Kevin shouted above the drone of the engine.

She followed the direction of his finger and there, grazing contentedly, was a huge herd of elephants. As the plane dropped from the sky some of the animals looked up inquisitively before continuing to pluck their food from among the grasses.

The solitary figure of a man grew clearer as the aircraft neared the tiny, low building that seemed out of place in the wilderness below. When they finally touched down on the primitive runway, the man disappeared, returning moments later driving a Land-Rover.

'One of the safari vehicles. There should be more on the way,' Kevin said snapping free of the seat belt and turning to loosen Nancy's.

On the ground, he greeted the safari driver before they walked away to join Della. The three stood a few yards away in a huddle, checking the names of the tourists going on safari. John appeared at Nancy's side, seized their bags and, without a word, led the way to the shade of the outbuilding. Nancy and the excited group followed. Nervously, she looked around the wasteland that stretched on all sides as far as the eye could see.

'What shall we do if the other vehicles don't turn up? Kevin said there should be others.'

Her voice trembled as she looked at John and his frown melted as he began to chuckle.

'There's transport laid on. They'll have seen the plane land and be along soon. Kevin will have radioed a message.'

Just then, Nancy saw a spiral of dust rapidly drawing closer. The sun glinted on the windscreen of the leading Land-Rover as it turned through a gap in the undergrowth and bore down on them, slowing to a stop in a trail of dust, only a few yards from where they stood. Another vehicle stopped a short distance behind.

Della stepped forward and ushered

her clients into the Land-Rovers. Within moments they were seated and the sturdy vehicles moved off, creating a grey cloud of rising dust. The remaining young Kenyan driver waved for the four of them to get in and, scrambling inside, they were soon speeding through the bush on to a rutted track that eventually led to a more recognisable road.

On one side, a vast lake shimmered and dazzled in the sunshine. On the far banks a pink cloud of flamingo trembled in a haze rising from the still water. The driver pointed to a mound near the bank and as they looked, the shape moved and the gigantic proportions of a hippopotamus, flanked by two calves, emerged from the murky depths.

A signpost indicated the Lodge Hotel was only a few minutes away. As the vehicle swerved along the road, Della leaned over and called out for Nancy's benefit, 'We'll be stopping there for coffee before we go on safari. I'm sure you'd like to freshen up. I know I would.'

At the landing strip, Della had positioned herself next to John and she now wrapped her arm in his in an affected gesture of pleasure. The Lodge Hotel was like a sprawling estate, a jewelled oasis in the shelter of tall trees. Inside, they were greeted by the reception clerk.

'I hope you have an enjoyable stay. You have cottages number twenty-seven and twenty-eight.'

John took the keys, throwing them into the air and catching them in a deft hand before picking up the bags.

'We know the way, thanks,' he said.

Kevin seized his and Della's bag, leaving the courier carrying her briefcase as she and Nancy followed. The path wound through an avenue of pink bougainvillea to a series of tiny bungalows dotted in the compound.

The hum of the air-conditioning greeted them in the coolness of the room, darkened by curtains drawn against the sun. A sliding partition separating two sleeping areas was partly open. John threw the keys on to the nearest bed and looked from Nancy to Della.

'Do these sleeping arrangements suit you or did you have anything else in mind?'

Nancy sensed an edge of bitterness in his voice and, outraged at his remark, refused to meet his eyes, glancing at Della instead. She was repairing her make-up in front of the mirror and raised her eyebrows as she looked at them through the glass.

'We can sort all that out later.'

She snapped her compact shut, turning with a questioning expression. Nancy shrugged and crossed to the bed at the other side of the room, dropping her bag on the turned-back sheets.

'Let's go for coffee then we can pick up a vehicle to take us around the reserve,' John suggested.

Nancy selected sunglasses, camera and a linen hat from her luggage, throwing them into a shoulder bag. John pulled a battered khaki hat from his bag and put it on at a jaunty angle, chuckling as he waited for an approving nod. He rummaged through his luggage for a pair of binoculars and threw them into a haversack that was already bulging.

They walked through the gardens to the main buildings. After they'd revived from the flight over a cup of coffee, John glanced at the others.

'Ready?'

He moved to the door and Della was swiftly at his side, plucking the sleeve of his shirt.

'I hope you don't mind Kevin and me tagging on like this,' she pouted disarmingly. 'Usually we laze around the pool while the tourists enjoy their outing but today will make a welcome change.'

John shook his head, but his features failed to respond. Nancy was in no doubt that he was far from pleased by the presence of either Della or Kevin.

She was puzzled by his attitude. If he and Della were as close as she had intimated, then it would have been a natural reaction for him to betray some sign of pleasure.

Outside in the driveway, their driver introduced himself as Peter and signalled for them to climb into the Land-Rover. Nancy stood back as John opened the door for Della, pulling the seat aside. Kevin was pressured into taking the place beside her in the rear. John's mouth twitched with a slow smile as he offered a hand to Nancy who sat behind the driver. John watched her in the mirror.

'Hand rails up there,' the driver said and pointed.

Nancy glanced at the open roof where sturdy metal bars made two separate compartments for the passengers to hold as they travelled over the rough terrain and stood to view the animals. John, who had ensured his seat alongside Nancy, demonstrated the procedure as the vehicle moved off, quickly gathering speed as it left the hotel compound.

Nancy tingled with excitement. After a few minutes of speeding along the open road, the air cooled inside the vehicle and she sat back to enjoy the adventure. By now, they were in the open bush and the firmer ground of the track was rapidly disappearing.

John slid his arm round Nancy's shoulders, steadying her against his chest. She looked up at him and smiled, her eyes bright with excitement and anticipation as the sun, directly over-head, relentlessly dazzled from a clear blue sky. Slowly the driver brought the vehicle to a halt.

'Over there,' he pointed.

Across the plain, the willowy necks of giraffes blended with the slender trunks of a clump of trees as they nibbled the succulent leaves of the topmost branches. Slowly they ambled from tree to tree in their search of food. Nancy took John's hand as he helped her to stand in the cramped vehicle, eagerly accepting the binoculars which she glued to her eyes for several minutes, enjoying the spectacle.

At a signal from the driver, they sat down and moved off, slowing for several minutes as a herd of zebra thundered across in front of them. As they drove through the cloud of dust sent up by the animals' hooves, Nancy peered through the window until the hovering murk shifted and the view ahead was clear.

'Look!' she yelled, jumping up in her seat to hang over the bars in the roof. 'Elephants!'

The herd of elephants picked their way majestically through the tall grasses. The great bull leader shook his massive head, flapping enormous frayed ears as he raised his trunk, seeming to signal the others forward. Cows with their sturdy calves meandered in the wake of the males, their tiny eyes darting around as they trudged behind their leaders.

'What a magnificent sight,' Nancy cried.

'I hope we see some of the big cats,' John said looking around through the binoculars. 'They should be coming down from the dry areas looking for food. If it was the rainy season we'd be out of luck. They have all the food they need then, no need to travel.'

'Wise beasts,' Della muttered from the back.

Nancy sat down as the driver moved off once again. Looking over her shoulder she smiled at Della.

'I suppose it's not the same when you've seen it all before,' she said, excusing the other girl's lack of enthusiasm. 'But you must admit it's a magnificent sight, seeing it for the first time.'

'Just show me a long, cool drink and I'll tell you what fires me,' Della pouted. 'We should be getting back to the lodge for lunch soon. I think I'll give the afternoon session a miss.'

John sighed and nudged Nancy's arm, winking as she caught his eye. She smiled.

'What about you, Kevin? Will you be joining us later?' John asked.

'I think Kevin would be more relaxed by the pool with me, wouldn't you, darling? And you have the flight back details to check.'

Della leaned forward to seize his arm, showing her first enthusiasm of the day. John grinned sympathetically as Kevin shrugged his shoulders, finding himself in a quandary about how to reply to Della's obvious demand for his company.

The vehicle slowed again and the driver motioned them ahead. Some yards away a cheetah lay in the undergrowth, guarding a kill.

'We're just too late to see the chase,' the driver explained. 'The cheetah is very dangerous now. He fears his food will be taken away if we go nearer.'

He slowly backed the Land-Rover, its wheels skimming as he turned the vehicle at an angle. With the engine still running, they viewed silently for a few minutes as the cheetah eyed them suspiciously. Nancy shivered.

'They only kill when they're hungry, to survive,' John explained, slipping his arm round her shoulders. 'It hasn't always been like this. Hunters used to come to Kenya and kill just for trophies to mount on their walls. Even today poachers stray on to the reserves in search of ivory or to trap animals.'

'In spite of the Rangers?' Nancy asked incredulously.

John's lip curled.

'It's big business, and dangerous for anyone who gets in the way. The poachers are desperate and terrorise some of the tribes to help. Cattle are lost and these people have to live from the land and what their herds provide. So, you can see it's not an easy problem to solve.'

Nancy was awed by the emotion he conveyed. It was obvious his love of Kenya was a powerful passion. Stern-faced, he stared across the land as they bumped over the grassy track. His voice interrupted her thoughts.

'Unchecked, the poachers could cause extinction on a large scale. The various authorities and governments do what they can but the problem's so immense throughout the continent, that it's a never-ending struggle. The Rangers are kept busy covering a great deal of territory.'

John sighed, looking at her.

'The people here are poor and the temptation to make money, the chance of even a few shillings makes a difference. Some of the Rangers are not trustworthy for the same reason.'

Travelling on across the plain, they disturbed large troops of baboons. Families wandered together stopping to groom each other as they watched the progress of the Land-Rover in their domain. They were now taking an interest in the Land-Rover and its passengers and one jumped on to the bonnet when they stopped for a moment.

'Make sure your windows are closed,' the driver called. 'I'll move off if it tries to get to the open roof.'

'They can be vicious if aroused,' John said watching the baboon picking at its matted pelt as it leered at them from its perch.

'Can't we all,' Della said cuttingly.

The baboon loped from the front of the vehicle on to the gritty surface of the track and the driver took the opportunity to move off rapidly. Leaving the clearing, they sped through a clump of trees. The driver rapidly changed gear as a herd of zebra galloped towards them. The animals suddenly veered to one side as the leaders caught sight of the approaching vehicle. The young Kenyan driver tried to avoid a collision by spinning the driving wheel in the opposite direction but it was too late.

Some of the fleeing zebras glanced the side of the Land-Rover, rocking it precariously at a dangerous angle. The driver spun the wheel frantically, failing to see the spiky trunk of a dead tree half hidden in the undergrowth. There was a grinding of metal as the chassis of the vehicle scraped the upearthed roots of the tree then a resounding hiss as the Land-Rover jolted to a stop.

They were shaken like rag dolls inside the vehicle, momentarily stunned by the impact as they scrambled to extricate themselves from between the backs of the seats. Nancy trembled uncontrollably, easing herself from the floor.

'Are you all right?'

She leaned over John who was rubbing his forehead.

'Just a slight bump. I'm OK. What about you?'

She nodded, turning to look into the back when Della began to moan.

'I'm all right. Just torn my blouse.'

Kevin flexed his shoulders, raising himself on to the seat.

'What about Peter, the driver?'

The young Kenyan was slumped over the wheel, his head over at an awkward angle.

7

John scrambled across the back of the seat and leaned over the inert driver, feeling for a pulse in his neck.

'I think he's OK. Probably knocked unconscious on impact and most likely hit his head on the dashboard.'

Kevin climbed from the back and leaned inside helping John lay the injured Kenyan along the seat. Peter moaned slightly as they moved him. His brow was grazed and blood trickled down his face.

'Hand me the haversack,' John asked.

Nancy retrieved it from the floor and John delved inside, bringing out a plastic bottle of water. Moistening his handkerchief, he dabbed Peter's face before handing the bottle to Nancy.

'Have a drink, one quick swallow, and pass it round.'

She gulped, not realising the extent

of her thirst until the lukewarm water filled her dry mouth. Della accepted the bottle eagerly and after drinking, splashed some on her cheeks.

'Go easy, Della. You don't know how long we're going to be here and there's no bar handy,' Kevin said lightly, trying to ease the tension.

'Don't worry,' John said. 'We'll soon be on our way.'

He slammed the passenger door and walked to the driver's side, easing the Kenyan's legs out of the way as he squeezed into the driver's seat. He turned the ignition key. There was a deathly silence as the others held their breath willing the engine to start.

'Come on, come on.'

John gritted his teeth trying to start the engine once more but there was no response, just the sickening metallic grating noise of the key in the ignition. Kevin beckoned him to the front of the vehicle and they squatted to look underneath.

'There's the damage.'

John pointed to the last drips of water draining from the tank.

'A great gash. See the twisted metal?'

He pulled aside low, sprawling branches to take a better look then gave a low whistle.

'Look at this,' he exclaimed.

The rear wheel of the Land-Rover had slipped into a trench where discoloured tusks of ivory lay hidden under foliage strategically placed to cover the hoard. Kevin gasped, turning to face him.

'There's no way of telling how long this has been here.'

'Or when they'll be coming back to collect it,' John said quietly.

'We'd better not be here when they do. There's a fortune buried here,' Kevin whispered. 'What shall we tell the girls?' he said hoarsely. 'There's no chance of getting this thing started. We'll have to go for help, or take our chances on foot.'

John nodded, looking around.

'Too dangerous for all of us and

there's the driver to think of. Even if he comes round there's every possibility he's concussed. No way could he walk, especially in this heat. We'll have to leave Nancy and Della to look after him while we go for help.'

'And if the poachers come back in the meantime, what then? What'll happen to the girls?'

'What else can we do?'

'One of us should stay with them.'

John pulled the foliage aside to examine the ivory.

'It's yellowing and covered with a film of soil. These freak winds that crop up from time to time in the bush could have covered it. It looks to me as if it's been buried for a while. I think we should take a chance and leave the girls here.'

Kevin frowned.

'I guess you're right. What else can we do?'

John eyed the Land-Rover's open roof.

'If baboons venture this way, the girls may be in trouble. We can't secure that.

Even if we could, they'd melt with the heat. It's going to be pretty uncomfortable as it is.'

He let the binoculars rest on his chest and frowned.

'Luckily we haven't seen any lions or big cats nearby. Let's hope they're farther up country.'

Their attention was distracted when Della jumped out, banging the door. Startled birds rose from their perch nearby in a cloud of frenzied wings. Della stretched then eased her blouse from the waistband of her skirt, tying the ends loosely.

'Much cooler,' she pouted. 'How long do you think we'll be here before they find us?'

John tactfully evaded the question, offering the bottle to Nancy who shook her head. His arm rested lightly on her shoulder, his fingers squeezing her flesh as he tried to reassure her.

'The radio! Shouldn't he be carrying a radio for this kind of emergency?' Kevin said suddenly.

He pulled the door open and searched the driver's seat, his hands frantically scrabbling around the floor. After a few moments he withdrew a battered radio and began to fumble with the controls. Turning it over he swore under his breath. He handed it to John who shrugged, feeling the dent where the radio had been crushed under the seat when they crashed.

'I don't suppose he carries a spare. I'll have another look.'

Kevin searched the floor without success then looked in the glove compartment.

'Look!'

He had a revolver in a suede case. He pulled it out and examined it.

'It's loaded. Five rounds.'

John took the weapon and checked it, slipping it in the waistband of his trousers.

'Have another look in the glove compartment, for spare bullets.'

Nancy leaned back in the seat. Her face was white, her eyes moist and luminous as she began to realise the danger they faced. She pressed her lips together, biting back her rising fear.

'What are we going to do?' she said.

John leaned into the Land-Rover.

'It's best if you and Della stay with Peter. He should come round soon.'

'And what about you?'

'Kevin and I will go for help. With a bit of luck we might come across one of the other safari vehicles. If not, we should make the lodge before long then we'll get someone out with another vehicle.'

'Will you be all right?' Nancy asked. 'Will you be able to find your way?'

She turned her head from side to side, gazing at the scrubland that looked the same wherever the eyes rested.

'John has a sense of direction better than a homing pigeon. We'll be OK,' Kevin replied.

They both took a long drink from the water bottle, pulled on their hats and prepared to leave.

116

'Keep your doors closed all the time,' John said sternly, looking at Della. 'And don't get out of the vehicle. If you see the baboons, frighten them by blowing the horn. The other animals won't come near you. We'll be as quick as we can. Try not to worry. You'll be all right if you do as we've said.'

He looked at Nancy, forcing a smile as, reluctantly, he turned away with Kevin and trudged off.

Nancy's shoulders tensed as she looked around. The landscape, grim, deserted and barren, matched the wretched, sickening emptiness in her heart now that John had gone. Della stood up and leaned on the roof bars. Nancy joined Della, standing to peer over the top of the vehicle, gulping in the fresh air as she scanned the horizon. The sun was directly overhead, beating down relentlessly from a cloudless sky.

Pangs of hunger gnawing at her stomach reminded her it was ages since she'd eaten. She sat down and fumbled in her bag, her spirits soaring when her fingers closed round a tube of sweets.

'Have one, Della. It might help the thirst go away.'

'And the hunger,' Della added. 'I'm starving.'

'Let's hope no-one out there is,' Nancy said apprehensively.

'I'm applying for a transfer to some civilised place like Spain or Greece as soon as I'm out of this mess. If I ever get out of this mess,' Della added in a more subdued voice.

'John will get help, you'll see. We'll see another Land-Rover appear before long.'

'Huh!' Della curled her lip. 'It would take Superman to get to the lodge in this heat. The lions'll be hunting, too. They'll be lucky to get far without using that gun. Perhaps we'll hear them fire.'

Della flopped down in the back seat, cradling her knees.

'Our best bet would be to hoot that horn until someone hears us,' she said looking to the front where the driver,

Peter, still lay unmoving and breathing heavily.

Nancy peered over the back of the seat.

'I'll try giving him another sip of water.'

She gave Della the bottle after carefully tipping some into the cap. Easing the Kenyan's head, she trickled a few drops into his slack mouth.

'I think he's moving. He's coming round.'

Della clambered over the seat and they both stared as the driver gently eased his limbs. He moaned slowly and raised a hand to his head, trying to lift himself from the seat.

'No,' Nancy said quietly. 'Lie still for a moment. You've been knocked out. Take it easy.'

His eyes opened at the sound of her voice and he quickly glanced around.

'We crashed . . . the zebras were stampeding . . . '

His eyes closed and he muttered under his breath before slowly raising himself to a sitting position.

'Where are the others?' he asked.

'They've gone for help,' Della said quickly.

Peter reached for the radio lying on the floor.

'It's broken,' Nancy said, 'but they've taken your gun.'

'And the spare bullets,' Della added.

'How long ago?'

'About an hour . . . maybe longer,' Nancy said and Della nodded.

Peter opened the door and tottered out, testing his legs unsteadily on the uneven ground. Shielding his eyes from the glaring sun he called, 'Which way?'

Della pointed.

'Over there.'

He nodded slowly and looked ahead.

'A little way on there's a settlement. Just small village. We make for it. Safer than Land-Rover especially after dark.'

'Surely we'll be out of here by then,' Della exclaimed.

'Darkness falls quickly in the tropics,

missy. Best be safe, eh?'

'But John said we should stay here,' Nancy protested opening the door and climbing out. 'What if they send help and we're gone?'

'Ranger will know.'

Nancy and Della looked at one another. Peter reached into the vehicle for his hat and a stout stick he carried under the seat. He withdrew a massive hunting knife in a leather case which he slotted in his belt.

Slamming the door, he beckoned them to follow, setting out over the rough grass and broken stumps, his unsteady footsteps betraying the fact that he had still not completely recovered from the accident. After a moment's hesitation, Nancy shoved the bottle of water into her bag and nodded to Della.

'We'd better do as he says. I don't want to stay here on my own.'

They followed Peter, stumbling over clumped grasses, searching for sight of the settlement he'd mentioned. Soon, their clothes were sticking to their skin like wet rags. They'd walked for nearly two hours when Peter stopped, waiting for the girls to draw abreast.

They each sank on to their knees in front of him, too breathless to speak. Nancy reached for the water bottle and held it up, peering through the pale plastic. Only drops remained. She offered it to Peter who shook his head, nodding towards Della. The courier took it with a thin smile.

'Thanks.'

She drained the bottle before throwing it aside.

'Not far now, missies. Over the crest we see huts of Masai village.'

Without further words, he turned and strode on and the two girls were obliged to follow. Climbing over the dusty ridge, they were relieved to see a cluster of thatched huts encircled by a crude fencing.

'Masai village,' Peter said with a grin.

His steps quickened to a run down the other side of the ridge and the girls, momentarily forgetting their fatigue, trotted after him. Children emerged from the gateway, waving and jumping excitedly with shrill cries. They were joined by tall warriors, clutching spears and shields which they shook above their heads. Nancy and Della looked at one another in alarm.

'They don't look very friendly,' Della hissed.

The Masai came to meet them. Tall and impressive in red cloaks, they wore strings of beads wound tightly round the smooth ebony of their necks. Strange white symbols and patterns were daubed on exposed flesh. Their aloof dignity struck a chord of fear in the two girls when they found themselves being examined by several sets of eyes. The warriors looked at Nancy and Della with blatant interest, chattering among themselves.

Nancy trembled when a group of women surrounded her, forming a barrier with their arms. Their shrill, excited cries resounded in her ears to an almost deafening pitch. She tried to resist their urgent fingers as they struggled to pull her inside the enclosure of the village. Tugging at her clothes, they grasped her wrists and pulled until she was compelled to follow. Peter watched with a huge grin, indicating that the girls should go with the Masai.

'Food.' He chuckled. 'They give you food.'

By now Nancy was inside the enclosure of the village. A fire glowed in the central area where a row of blackened pots and pans stood simmering on the glowing embers. Della flashed a worried look at Nancy, eyeing the fire with its cooking implements.

'I only hope we're not on the menu.'

Nancy frowned, willing her to be quiet. Once inside the safety of the village, the women ushered the girls in a friendly fashion, smiling and patting their arms as they compared the whiteness of their skin to the gleaming lustre of their own. Nancy smiled as a young girl kneeled to touch her shoes, now soiled, dusty and worn from their long trek over the plain.

The girl motioned Nancy and Della to follow into the darkness of one of the huts. It was cool inside, the only light filtering through the gaping mouth of the door. Beds of grasses lay on the floor and the girl waved, indicating that the two should rest. Nancy sank down with a sigh, cradling her head on her knees.

'What a relief,' she breathed, smiling at the girl who hurried outside, giggling as she withdrew.

Nancy lay back on the softness of the dried foliage, moaning at the comfort as she relaxed. Three giggling girls returned with crude bowls of steaming stew. The appetising smell filled the confined space.

Nancy's lips watered and she eagerly accepted a bowl from the smiling Masai girl who offered a spoon of sorts, giggling as she held a hand to her mouth and slid out of the door to join her companions who were peeping inside. Della's bowl lay on the floor by the mattress where she perched gingerly on a corner. Beside it lay two mugs and a pitcher of frothy milk. She poured the milk, handing a mug to Nancy who drained the vessel before setting it down.

'Mmm, delicious. I'm going to try this.'

Nancy picked up the bowl and ate greedily.

'Try it, Della. It's good.'

Della hovered on the brink of indecision but after a few moments, picked up her portion and began to eat ravenously. Daylight was fading from the doorway as the sunlight lessened and the rosy glow from the compound fire cast lengthening shadows that streaked by the open doorway.

Della sat hugging her knees. She hadn't spoken for several minutes and Nancy knew Della was desperately afraid.

'John and Kevin will be coming soon.

They'll have reached the lodge and there'll be a party looking for us. The Ranger will know we're at the village, Peter said so. Why don't you try to get some rest, Della?'

Nancy's eyelids felt heavy. Comfortable and drowsy now she'd eaten, she stretched on the grass mattress and was soon lost to sleep.

8

A shrill scream bounced from wall to wall in the pitch black darkness of the tiny hut. Nancy sprang up, limbs tense and flesh prickling with an unknown terror. Night had fallen and only the flickering flames of the fire illuminated the compound outside.

The screaming began again then quietened to a choking sob. Nancy, remembering Della, looked around to locate the other mattress.

'Della, where are you?'

'I'm here. Someone came in here then left. What are they going to do?'

Nancy sat down beside Della and put her arm around Della's shoulders. She was shaking, her body moist and clammy, bathed in a film of sweat.

'It's all right, Della. They were probably bringing more food. We can't come to any harm. Haven't they taken care of us since we arrived?'

'Why doesn't the Ranger come? Maybe John and Kevin never made it.'

She choked on a sob.

'They'll probably leave first thing in the morning. It's too dark for them to find us until daybreak. Until then you should try to sleep.'

Nancy's patience was wearing thin. She wondered how Della came to be a representative of Tropical Dream Holidays when her resourcefulness so easily vanished. In the hotel, she dealt competently with her clients but now, when character and stamina were being tested, Della's poise had disintegrated making her into a feeble apology of her former self.

'As soon as we're out of this I'm transferring to another resort.'

'You must have been happy when you first came,' Nancy began.

'It seemed rosy enough but John was the attraction that kept me here.'

Nancy tensed, willing her to go on.

'I thought he and I had something

but all John has is . . . is Kenya. He can't see past this damn country. This is his only love.'

Nancy was silent, her thoughts running riot.

'So if you think you have something going with John,' she went on, 'I warn you, just be sure you know what you're getting into,' Della snorted, covering her face with both hands. 'He'll never leave this land.'

'It's his home,' Nancy said quietly.

'His prison more like,' Della growled. 'He'll still be here in a hundred years, picking a living from this wilderness. No-one with any sense could take that on.'

Nancy gave the girl a final hug, before picking the way to her own bed. As she stretched on the mattress, Della's words came back to haunt her.

'*Maybe John and Kevin never made it back to the lodge. Perhaps something happened to them.*'

Had they fallen into some danger, or even got lost on the vast plain? She shivered, thinking of John and Kevin in the wilderness of Amboseli. Without shelter and only a revolver between them, they would be at the mercy of marauding, ferocious animals. Could they survive until morning?

'What made you come to Kenya?' Della's voice reached her through the darkness.

Nancy hesitated.

'We'd planned it for ages. At one time I thought it might be our honeymoon, but things went sour and I came on my own.'

'And now,' Della was saying. 'What are you going to do now?'

Nancy shifted on the mattress and sat up, facing Della's shadowy figure.

'Get on with life, I suppose. It was all for the best. I'm beginning to see that now.'

'Since you met John?'

Nancy held her breath, wishing she could see the other girl's face.

'I hardly know him. What makes you think he features in my plans?'

'That's all right then. It would be too bad to be hurt again. John won't be here much longer, you see. He has plans.'

'Yes, he told me.'

The words were out before Nancy realised and she wished she had bitten her tongue as her reply caused a further rustling of Della's mattress.

'What exactly did he tell you?'

The voice was firmer yet there was a trace of anxiety in the tone.

'He said he wanted to join his father in Kericho on the tea plantations, get out of the hotel business.'

There was silence for a moment before Della went on.

'That old dream,' she said scornfully. 'I've been trying to talk him out of that for ages. I told him we could move to a better climate. He's a wizard in management and with my skills we would be a hit wherever we went. He's determined to find someone . . . anyone . . . to go with him. Must have healthy sons to work alongside me, he says.'

132

She laughed, but the sound was hollow and without mirth.

'I think all he needs is a brood mare.'

She paused and sighed again.

'He really is keen on the Kericho idea, I know. But I keep telling him, where would he get all his diversions if he was away from the hotel business. He won't find so many willing young females up country.'

Nancy knew Della was waiting for a reaction but remained silent as the words tore a sickening hole in her heart. John had been playing a game with her. She saw it clearly now. Kevin had said Della and John were an item. It was obvious they still were. Nancy's cheeks burned through the darkness, realising she had been no more than one of John's diversions.

The grasses rustled on Della's bed and Nancy hoped she had lain down. She'd heard enough. Her heart was beating rapidly as anger consumed every inch of her being. But rising with the rage was the pain of betrayal as she remembered John's kisses, the soft and tender touch of his hands and the passion in his eyes when he told her he loved her. Nancy listened to the regular breathing that meant Della was finally asleep.

Nancy awoke to see it was almost daybreak. Della still slept, curled into a ball on the grassy bed. There was movement outside and the fire was crackling with fresh kindling. Through the gap of the door, she saw figures crossing to and fro carrying cooking pots and a variety of implements.

She rose and tip-toed to the door, not wanting to rouse Della. Peeping outside, her eyes skimmed the surroundings until they came to rest on figures squatting around the fire, cradling mugs in their hands. They were engrossed in conversation with much waving of hands and quiet laughter.

Nancy stepped outside and walked slowly across the compound towards the little group huddled around the fire. Riddled with uncertainty, she hesitated, unsure whether or not she should go back inside the hut until someone summoned her but it was too late. She had been spotted. A cry of recognition erupted and arms pointed her way.

Someone stood up, a tall, muscular figure in khaki trousers with a brimmed hat pushed back on his head. He pushed both hands into his pockets, addressing the others who followed him with their eyes as he moved around the fire.

'Ah, so you are ready to travel.'

Nancy hesitated, waiting for him to go on, her mind racing with confused emotions. Where were John and Kevin? Who was this man? He was addressing her again and by now stood facing her.

'Where is the other girl? Still asleep?'

Nancy nodded.

'I'll wake her.'

She turned to retrace her steps but her arm was seized.

'Leave her. We'll make off at day-break.'

'Where are John and Kevin, and

Peter, the driver?'

He ignored the questions, leading her to the fringe of the group by the fire. A mug of hot liquid was pressed into her hand and as she drank, she looked at the newcomers. There was the one who'd spoken and three Africans in drill shorts and T-shirts. They sat between the Masai warriors who were strangely quiet.

'Where is the safari driver, Peter?' she asked again.

The tall man chuckled.

'No doubt still asleep, like your friend.'

His companions grinned at the words and as Nancy's eyes flashed from one to the other, she knew something was wrong. Their expressions were evil as the flickering flames threw moving shadows across their faces. Her flesh crept with discomfort as she watched them and she cringed with fear when she saw a revolver stuck in the belt of the man who'd spoken.

Words were exchanged across the fire

but the strange tongue was unintelligible and Nancy's worry grew swiftly. Her fear intensified when the tall man stood up, summoning the others.

'We'll leave now.'

He nodded in Nancy's direction and she watched, horror stricken as two of the Kenyans came swiftly towards her with outstretched hands. She backed away but their leader halted her retreat when strong fists grabbed her by the shoulders. The mug fell to the ground, the liquid sizzling as it splashed on to the fire. Bitter panic rose, and her eyes flashed to the Masai pleading for help but no-one moved.

Her whimpering grew louder until her screams reverberated across the compound. A foul-smelling hand was clamped across her mouth and she was dragged away. Trailing her heels, she twisted and struggled but she was powerless, the only result of her efforts, a vicious scratch across her forearm.

'Keep quiet or we'll take your friend, too, and dump you both in the lions feeding ground.'

The words were snarled into her ear as the hand slithered from her mouth. She gulped for air, thoughts running riot. Where were they taking her? What was going to happen to Della and Peter? She hadn't seen him round the fire with the others. As if in answer to her questions, the tall man bundled her into the back of a Land-Rover outside the compound.

'Your friends can pass on the information when they come looking for you. Keep out of our way or you'll be pickings for the vultures.'

The others took up his mirthless chuckle as they clambered into the vehicle, one on either side of her and the other in front, turning round in the seat to leer at her discomfort. Nancy knew Della was safe but what about Peter? She had to know.

'What have you done to the Kenyan?'

'He's OK. Trussed like a chicken but he'll deliver the message all right. The Masai'll have him free by now.'

Dawn was lightening the horizon with its myriad of colours, changing as rapidly as a magic lantern. The sky, streaked with colours, was too vivid to be real. But as Nancy's terrified eyes darted from side to side, she was unaware of the beauty, her only thought, what was going to happen next?

9

Nancy's watch had been wrenched from her wrist in the struggle but the sun, rising over the distant hills, gave her some sense of time. Despite her discomfort and the anxiety of what was to happen next, she wondered how Della fared. Had John and Kevin returned? She glanced back, hoping to see a spiral of dust marking the progress of a pursuing vehicle.

Since they'd set off, Nancy had learned the leader's name was Denzil. His English was heavily accented though she was unable to place the strange drawl, Australian or maybe South African, she thought.

The white man and his companions had made themselves at home in the Masai compound but she'd sensed they were unwelcome. Nancy could not understand why the friendly Masai, witnesses to her distress, had done nothing to help. She was loath to ask questions, fearing their answers. Did they mean to hold her for ransom? But what for?

The sun was high but Nancy shivered. Everything had happened so quickly. She wished she would wake up and find it all to have been a nightmare. The Land-Rover stopped abruptly, jolting Nancy into a terrified awareness. She sat stiffly, watching the others tumble out and pull aside the branches of a clump of sprawling trees. The chassis of another vehicle emerged and one of the Kenyans climbed into the driver's seat. After a few choking coughs, the engine roared into life and the man drove it into full view. They were off again, with the second Land-Rover on their tail.

They climbed a hill, skimming down the other side. Nancy saw the abandoned safari wagon lying where they had left it, a few hundred yards ahead. She trembled, wondering what they would find. Had John and Kevin returned to look for them and been ambushed by these desperate men?

Disregarding the fear for her own safety, she was relieved to find the damaged vehicle deserted when they ground to a halt, raising a cloud of dust. Nancy winced when the men jumped out, slamming the doors. The men tied a tow rope to the Land-Rover, pulling it free of the tangle of roots that had crippled the vehicle when they crashed. She watched them scrabbling among the undergrowth. Huge branches and uprooted bushes were hurled aside, exposing a cavity.

Two of the Kenyans lowered themselves into the hole, cursing when their feet slipped, while their companions watched from the rim, shouting instructions. Eventually, they hauled huge tusks of ivory from beneath the spot where the Land-Rover had stood at its crazy angle. Nancy looked on in horror, remembering what John said about ivory poachers and for the first time, realised the extent of her predicament. They would never set her free now. She was a witness and could identify them to the authorities.

Her head swam and she lurched on the seat, trembling as she waited to be dragged outside. She listened to the rasping voices yelling as they piled the ivory into the second Land-Rover. Great tusks stuck up through the open roof like gigantic fingers pointing to the sky. They made no effort to conceal the hoard and Nancy's heart pounded with renewed hope. Surely someone would see them. There were patrols on the lookout. John said they were always watching for poachers.

She considered leaping from the Land-Rover while the men were preoccupied and taking her chances on the plain. But how far would she get before they came after her, or put a bullet in her back? She hesitated, wondering if there might be a better chance of survival if she waited until they were distracted again, when they transferred the ivory.

Nancy's decision was resolved by the others. At a signal from Denzil, the men climbed into the two Land-Rovers, one with the driver of the second vehicle and the other in front with Denzil. Ahead lay an expanse of wooded land standing like an island on the plain. Denzil pulled off the track and the other vehicle followed slowly, under its heavy load.

The two drivers manoeuvred the vehicles out of sight from any chance traffic. Satisfied they were securely hidden, the men jumped out and huddled in animated conversation. Denzil beckoned one man to follow him to the Land-Rover where Nancy huddled, cringing with fear. Was this the end, she wondered, but to her surprise, Denzil climbed into the driver's seat with the other man beside him. He revved the engine into life and reversed through the trees, on to the track, leaving the others watching their progress.

'What's happening?' she cried. 'Why are you keeping me? Just let me go. What harm can I do?'

Her terrified voice rose shrilly above the grating noise of the engine, and Denzil eyed her through the mirror, a bitter grin distorting his features.

'You're our insurance, sweetheart. No-one's going to take any pot shots at us with you on board. Just behave yourself and we'll treat you all right.'

'Where are we going?' she cried, thumping a fist into Denzil's back.

Denzil leaned forward to dodge the blows, laughing loudly.

'I like a woman with spirit,' he said looking through the mirror. 'I'll tell you where we're going, then you can sit back like a good girl and enjoy the ride. Better than any safari and this one's free.'

His laughter shredded Nancy's nerves. She waited for him to go on but for a moment he concentrated on the uneven ground as the Land-Rover dipped precariously over pitted roots and scattered stones.

Over his shoulder he said, 'We're going to pick up a lorry I've left in the village ahead. It was too far into the bush to chance taking it to collect the stuff. The damn suspension would have gone.' He nodded to the Kenyan.

'He'll drive it back. And that'll leave you and me on our own, sweetheart. If you behave yourself we can make a detour on the way back. Get out and stretch your legs.'

His low, throaty chuckle left Nancy in no doubt about her fate. She brightened, remembering he had mentioned a village. There would be people . . . people she could run to . . . people who would help her. As if reading her thoughts, he glanced through the mirror again, staring into her eyes.

'Don't get any clever ideas. I'll be watching you all the time. One false move and I'll carve my initials on your pretty face. Not so pretty then, eh?'

They began to pass a scattering of thatched huts where children played in the dirt. Here and there tall warriors stood like statues, with red cloaks draped over thin shoulders, holding spears in clenched fists.

Nancy tried to attract their attention, waving her arms frantically but the Masai remained motionless, only their eyes reacting to the passing vehicle. After a few minutes the village came into view. The vehicle threaded its way slowly along the dust track that served as a main thoroughfare.

Nancy noticed that people went about their business, ignoring the advancing Land-Rover as if this was a usual occurrence in the village and remembered what John said. The chance of easy money, no matter how it was come by, was hard to turn away if there were starving children at home. And there was plenty of evidence here to support that.

The erratic chug of the engine stopped and the men jumped out.

Denzil seized Nancy's arm, his filthy, broken finger nails digging into her sore flesh.

'Get into the front and keep your mouth shut,' he snarled.

At that moment, the makeshift doors of a lean-to shed were cast aside and an open-backed lorry edged its way on to the road. She inched across the seat to the driver's door, clawing at the catch for a chance to escape but it was too late. Denzil stood outside. With a curse the door was wrenched from her hand, leaving her lying across the seat sobbing.

This was the end. How much longer had she? Denzil was back behind the wheel and they were leaving the village now. She must try again. She reached for the handle and turned it, twisting on the seat to swing her legs on to the ground.

Denzil jolted the Land-Rover to a halt with a screech of brakes. Leaning across, he yanked the door shut then grabbed her throat in a powerful fist, his foul breath in her face. Digging her nails into his arm she struggled until everything went scarlet. Black drifted into the red, blotting out reality . . .

10

Nancy's head exploded and her mouth filled with bile. Slipping uneasily into the present renewed the fear and despair, this time worsened by a sore throat and waves of nausea with the motion of the vehicle. Beside her, Denzil frowned, scanning the road ahead. He glanced sideways, curling his lips before looking away.

Nancy ventured to sit up. Her body ached and she'd strained her shoulder when attempting to open the door. Swallowing rapidly, she measured her breathing, then concentrated on the road.

The lorry was well ahead of them, only a trail of dust betraying its presence. A little way off the track lay the wooded area where the second Land-Rover waited. Denzil had it in his sights and it seemed to spur him on, taking only minutes to reach the spot. He jumped out, calling his companions.

The lorry was clearly visible from the track and he began to swear loudly, punctuating the names of the others with obscenities. He stomped to the cab and looked inside, pushing the battered hat from his brow impatiently.

Nancy sat up, craning her neck. The lorry was empty and the others nowhere to be seen. Only the cries of circling birds broke the eerie silence. Suddenly pandemonium broke loose. Branches were hurled aside and an army of uniformed Rangers, rifles at the ready, sprang into full view. Everyone seemed to be yelling at once, orders and threats delivered over rifle barrels. Denzil dropped to his knees, grabbing the revolver at his waist but before he could take aim, he was overpowered from behind and sent sprawling. Relief flooded Nancy and tears ran down her face as she tried to control her hysteria.

When the poachers were rounded up, she watched the Rangers manoeuvre the Land-Rover, bulging with ivory, out of its hiding place and on to the track where it was driven away under an armed escort. The four Kenyans, cowering with fear, were loaded into the back of the lorry with Denzil, struggling and yelling until he was overcome by force and thrown on board to join his fellow thieves.

A friendly Ranger offered Nancy a flask of water. She gulped the tepid liquid. The Ranger pulled on to the track and joined the cavalcade of vehicles now concealed by a fog of dust.

'Where are we going?' Nancy asked.

'To join your friends at the Masai. Not many minutes and you have food. Safe now missy. No problem.'

His wide, toothy smile filled her with more confidence than she had felt for hours.

The welcome sight of the village had her sitting erect, watching for the familiar figures she hoped would be there, waiting. The Ranger parked outside the compound and helped her down. Figures rose in greeting and someone called her name. It was John! He bounded forward, sweeping her into his arms, circling round and round.

'Oh, darling. Thank goodness you're safe. Did they hurt you?'

His fingers traced the bruise on her neck with a feather-like touch before his lips gently caressed the soreness.

'I'm all right. I was so worried about you . . . both of you,' Nancy gasped. 'I thought you might have got lost or those men might have found you.'

The memory of Della's traumatic statements and all that had happened evaporated in the joy of seeing him. Her words were lost in another kiss and as Nancy clasped her arms around his neck, she knew that she never wanted to let him go again. Despite everything, no matter what Della had insinuated, she had fallen in love with Kenya and with John.

Hand in hand, they walked to the warmth of the fire and she squatted in the comforting clasp of his arm. A mug of hot milk was pressed into her fist and she drank eagerly. Hesitantly, Nancy told what had happened from the moment she'd been dragged from the compound. The Masai looked on interrupting with questions in their strange dialect.

'They are asking me if you are my woman,' John explained.

Nancy felt her face glowing as she looked at him.

'I've told them yes.'

John bent to kiss her again and the excited warbling from the circle of onlookers registered their approval. Nancy gripped John's arm.

'Why didn't they come to help me when they saw those men taking me away?' she asked.

'They were afraid. The gang had the safari driver in one of the huts promising to kill him if they gave you an inkling of what was going on. They'd been threatened, too. The Masai live through their herds and the poachers threatened to slaughter every animal.

You know what that would mean to people like this. But you have them to thank for the Rangers being there. They sent runners to the station as soon as you'd left.'

Della came hurrying from the hut. She sank to her knees beside John and Nancy, ignoring the others.

'Thank heavens you're all right, Nancy. I had a fit when they hauled you off. I felt sure I'd be next.'

There was genuine concern on her face but it was briefly lived as she went on.

'John, how soon can you get us out of this nightmare?'

'We're safe. That's all that matters for now,' he replied.

'Well, all I can think of is a long, hot bath.'

She stood up, tapping her foot impatiently.

'It would be rude not to stay for food,' John said quietly. 'These are proud people. They've treated you with the utmost courtesy. Have the grace to conduct yourself with some of the dignity they've shown you.'

John spoke to the tribesmen in their own tongue. His words provoked a guffaw of laughter leaving no doubt that Della had been the butt of a joke. She sank down hurriedly beside Nancy who glanced at her, noting her distress. She squeezed Della's hand.

'We'll be back at the lodge soon then we can both have a nice, leisurely bath. Such bliss to look forward to. You'll feel better soon.'

The Masai women emerged from their huts busy with the preparation of food. It was a communal affair with families mingling together, squatting on the compound with bowls of meaty soup.

After the meal, they were soon on their way after a farewell that involved shaking every hand in the village. Nancy was overcome when the women pressed necklaces and bracelets of multi-coloured, intricate designs into her hand. They warbled approval as she wound the beads around her neck and wrists and thanked the smiling women. Della, too, accepted their gifts but shoved them into her bag with little ceremony.

The tribe gathered at the village boundary, waving until the Land-Rover was on the crest of the rise. John slid his arm around Nancy's waist and held her tightly. Safe in his arms, she remembered Della's words and wondered how much could she believe.

It was late afternoon when the lodge appeared in the distance, brightening their spirits with the glimpse of civilisation. Nancy began to share Della's sentiments, thinking of the leisurely, hot bath that would be her priority when they arrived. However, they were greeted by Kevin, seated on the terrace. By the time they reached his side, a tray of cold drinks was waiting. Della picked up her drink and drained the glass in one draught.

'Oh, that was great,' she said. 'Now, I'm off to find a tub.'

With that, she turned and left the others staring after her.

'I think I'll follow Della,' Nancy said, laying her glass on the table. 'A soothing bath sounds a great idea.'

She grinned as Kevin and John nodded in understanding, then followed Della, along the leafy avenue towards the bungalow.

The soothing drone of the air conditioner crooned its welcome. Nancy heard Della humming softly from the bathroom and set about selecting clean garments from her travelling bag while she waited for her to emerge. Della came out, wrapped in a white towel and flopped on to her bed.

'I feel almost human again,' she breathed, stretching on the sheets. 'Can't wait to get back to the Africana.'

Nancy smiled and padded into the bathroom. She stepped inside the shower cubicle and turned on the spray. It gushed into her face and she revelled in the assault of tepid water on her skin.

Stepping out she towelled herself dry before wrapping the fluffy white towel around her to venture into the other room. She gasped. Della had gone and John stood by the bed, undoing the buttons of his shirt.

'What are you doing here?' she cried, clutching the towel around her.

'The shower doesn't work next door and Della said I could follow you.'

He grinned.

'I'll only take a minute. Just a quick sluice and then change my shirt.'

He disappeared into the bathroom, returning minutes later dabbing his face. He snatched a T-shirt and shook it free of creases. Nancy was mesmerised by the smooth firm contours of his body, as he raised his arms to pull on the shirt.

He stepped forward, throwing aside the shirt, and pulled her into his arms. John's lips were cool as they descended on hers.

Someone at the door interrupted the blissful moment.

Outside on the footpath, the unmistakable voice of Della trilled in laughter as she chatted noisily to one of her clients. John snatched his shirt before making for the door.

'Later, my love,' he said. 'We seem destined to be interrupted.'

Later, Nancy sat opposite John and Kevin, each nursing long, cool drinks rattling with ice. There were questions she was burning to ask about what had happened when they left looking for help.

'We seemed to walk for miles,' Kevin said. 'Then we found a track.'

'Yes.' John nodded. 'We could have been going in circles if we hadn't come across that. We followed it then we saw the lake in the distance and we knew we were on the right course. It was nearly dark but the lights were on at the lodge and we made a beeline for them.'

John smiled ruefully.

'Unfortunately, it was too late to come out again. The Rangers advised us to wait until daybreak, and the rest you know.'

He leaned forward and grasped Nancy's hand.

'Thank God it all ended safely.'

'I'll toast to that.'

Kevin held out his drink and the others did the same, smiling at the chink of glass on glass.

'What a pity Della isn't here,' Nancy said glancing around. 'I'm sure she'll have cheered up by now. I wonder if I should go and seek her out.'

'If I know Della, she'll be packed and ready to leave. I bet the first thing she did was to burn the ear off someone on the telephone arranging a return.'

They were still chuckling when they heard the trill of Della's high-pitched laughter and the clip-clop of her shoes along the path.

'Hi, folks! Just called to say bye-bye. I'm picking up a ride to the coast. Enjoy the rest of your stay. I'd like to say it's been fun, but . . . '

She shrugged her shoulders and with

a brief wave and toss of her head was gone. The three looked at each other, testing out who should laugh first. Kevin won and his hearty laughter frightened the perching monkeys in the treetops above as they added their screeching protests to the noise of his merriment.

11

Nancy gazed out of the window as the Cessna circled the Amboseli airstrip. John snapped free of his seat belt and leaned over.

'I'm going to speak to Kevin. Back in a minute.'

Nancy thought how wonderful it would be to face the rest of her life with him, but the uncertain future rose to torment her. John's life in Kenya was a world apart from the orderly routine of an office which was all she knew. How could she adjust? He must be mad to think that she could. It was too much of a chance to take. She knew she loved him but was love enough? John needed a wife who could help build his dream in Kericho. She was a provincial mouse. Richard was right after all.

Nancy closed her eyes, trying to deflect the bitter tears before they began. John would find someone else — someone more suited to the pattern of his life. As for herself, she would throw herself into her work as she had done when she had broken with Richard. It was all a matter of time.

Time! The very word grated on her mind. She glanced at John, in spirited conversation with Kevin. The sound of their laughter went unnoticed with the constant hum of the Cessna's engines.

When the Cessna landed, the driver from the hotel eased from his parking space in the shade and stepped out of the vehicle. He waved enthusiastically, catching sight of John among the passengers alighting from the small craft.

'It's as if you were a long-lost friend,' Nancy said, smiling at John who returned the wave with as much gusto.

'I hope I am. The people who work for me are not just employees. Many of them are friends, like Mtombo here.'

He nodded towards the waiting driver.

'I brought him with me from Nairobi. I know his family. And he knows mine,' he added.

There was no doubting his sincerity and Nancy realised how little she knew about John and his life in Kenya. There was so much he had not told her. How could she expect to know him after two weeks? How could she imagine that he could love her after so short an acquaintance?

She wanted to believe him but their lives were so different. Perhaps it was loneliness that had made him set her aside from the other guests. Had he seen her unhappiness and recognised his own? She no longer accepted Della's assessment of his character. Biting her lip, she followed John to the car, leaving Kevin to organise his check on the Cessna and the paperwork that awaited him.

Nancy felt drained of emotion as they sped towards the hotel. The next few days would be a strain. She knew that as the end of her holiday approached, she must face up to reality. The rest, like the holiday, had been a wonderful dream.

The familiarity of the hotel seemed like home after the eventful safari. Nancy took it in at a glance — the excited cries of bathers in the pool and the refreshing noise of splashing water. She longed to have her first swim in days. The thought of cool water lapping at her skin made her tingle with anticipated pleasure. But hunger taunted her into seeking something to eat at the snack bar before she went to change.

'Me, too. I'm starving,' John said promptly when she voiced her intention. 'But first I'd better check if anything has arisen while I've been away. All I need are problems,' he added with a rueful grin as he turned away.

Nancy waited at the reception desk while he spoke to the clerk. She saw Della, now completely at ease in her usual surroundings as she clip-clopped across the floor. No longer the dishevelled and distressed girl from Amboseli, Della was the smart, neatly dressed Tropical Dreams courier once more. She smoothed her hair with a casual flick of her fingers.

'Nancy, I've great news. You have a visitor. His name is Richard and he says he's your fiancé.'

She waited for the information to register, raising her brows. Nancy was stunned, a jumble of words battling in her throat. Della's voice rippled in amused laughter as she went on.

'He's very anxious to see you. Quite a dish. How on earth could you have left him behind?'

Her face was wreathed in enigmatic smiles as she waited for some comment from the still silent Nancy. Nancy gasped, biting back words that wanted to be out. She knew Della was testing her reaction to the statement, delivered loudly with dramatic overtones and she fought to keep calm.

Before she recovered, John turned

from the desk and was at her elbow. She looked at him wordlessly, her expression as puzzled and questioning as his. Della glanced from one to the other with a tinge of amusement.

'Your fiancé is sitting by the pool. Such a charmer.'

She grinned as she turned to leave. John's face darkened as he glowered.

'What does this mean?' he asked. 'I thought it was over between you. That's what you said. Where do we go from here, Nancy? It seems you have another choice to make.'

She raised her shoulders feeling the cold chill creeping over her body, frowning as she spoke.

'I . . . I don't know.'

'Then when you decide, you'd better let me know.'

He turned abruptly, making for his office. Hesitating at the door, he looked back, throwing the words over his shoulder.

'I don't think you've been honest with me. What was I? A holiday prank to while away the time?'

His eyes were like cut glass, cold and brittle, glaring beneath lowered brows as he slammed the door behind him. Nancy stood alone. Her shoulders stiffened and her fingers curled into fists at her side. John's bitter words cut like a knife. Squaring her shoulders, she stepped on to the terrace and shielded her eyes, scanning the grounds for Richard. He leaped up from the sun lounger, bounding across the grass to meet her. Gathering her limp figure into his arms he poured kisses on her mouth.

'Oh, Nancy, darling,' he whispered. 'I've been a fool. Say you'll forgive me and we can pick up our lives where we left them. I can't live without you. I've tried but it's no use. It's you I want, Nancy. Why couldn't I see that before? I've been so blind.'

'We have a lot to talk about, Richard,' Nancy said, pushing him away gently with the palms of her hands. 'Please, don't,' she said firmly, frowning as she glanced around. 'People are watching.'

'I want everyone to know I love you, Nancy. I don't care any more what anyone says. It's just you and me from now on, believe me.'

His words pleaded monotonously, leaving Nancy drained of spirit and in a state of bewilderment.

She wanted to turn away and run, anywhere, just to be on her own, away from everyone, Richard most of all.

'We'd better go up to my room. We have to talk.'

She tried to disentangle herself from his grasp as she led the way indoors to the lift. As they waited for it to descend, Richard pulled her into his arms and kissed her again. As they stepped inside the lift and the doors began to close, Nancy noticed John standing at his office door. She wondered how long he had stood there. But as his eyes burned with undisguised fury, Nancy was in no doubt. He had seen their embrace.

Her heart was in torment with the look on his face. She would find no relief until she explained what had happened — why Richard had appeared unannounced. Somewhere, in the mist that enveloped her, Richard's insistent voice listed plans he had made for their future. The words were not registering as she wrapped her arms around herself like a protective shield, trying to blot out his presence.

When they reached the door he was saying, 'I'll give notice at the new job. They'll be glad to take me back at the old place considering all I did for them. We'll buy a house.'

He paused to turn the key, reaching for Nancy's hand to lead her into the room. Nancy stiffened in the doorway, resisting Richard's gentle tug.

'What's the matter? Something wrong?' he asked.

Nancy pulled her hand free of his and stepped inside the room, closing the door behind her. She looked at him squarely, surprising herself by the calmness that simplified her frantic racing thoughts.

'Everything is all right if it happens to be what you want. It was all right for you to go away and leave me because that's what you wanted to do. You never spared a thought about what I wanted.'

'I've said I'm sorry, Nancy. I shouldn't have acted the way I did.'

He stepped towards her but Nancy held up the palm of her hand to forestall him.

'Now you think you can come back into my life and pick up the pieces, because again, that's what you want. Have you once stopped to ask me what I want?'

Nancy's voice rose in exasperation as she stared at his consternation.

'But I've asked you to marry me.'

'And I'm saying no. I'm sorry, Richard.'

He sank on to the bed, burying his face in cupped hands.

'I've made such a mess of things. Can't you give me another chance?'

Nancy stared in disbelief. This was a Richard she barely recognised. Gone was his assured manner and the belligerent attitude that had often caused her distress. He had always made the decisions. She'd allowed him to dominate her life without realising it. When he had left to take up his new job, her confidence had been totally shattered.

But now it was over. Now she was voicing her own plans and for the first time she knew she was master of her own destiny, with a future that did not include Richard. Nancy crossed to the window and looked out. The monkeys leaped from the balcony on to the branches of an overhanging tree and she smiled. Life can be simple and beautiful, she thought, especially if you are free. She turned to look at Richard. He was staring at her as if looking at a stranger.

'It's for the best, Richard. I'm surprised I didn't realise before now that we want different things out of life. We can never find them together. Keep your job up North. You'll find someone else, I know. You have so much to offer.'

She knew her last remark was tinged with sarcasm but she didn't care any more what he thought. She just wanted him to go — now. She bent to pick up his travel bag she'd dropped on a chair.

'No need to move your things. I'm sure Della, the courier, will let me share her room for the next couple of days before we're due to leave. I'll collect my belongings later.'

Richard's eyes, mirrored with disbelief, followed her as she moved to the door. He sat unmoving, rigid on the edge of the bed. Nancy forced a weak smile.

'Goodbye, Richard,' and as she looked at him she knew the only feelings she had left for him were ones of pity.

Nancy couldn't leave things as they were between John and herself now. His accusations festered and the wound wouldn't heal until she had explained. She owed it to herself to put matters straight. Descending to the foyer, she waited at the reception desk, making an

174

effort to pluck up the courage to ask for him.

New guests were signing the hotel register on their arrival. Their excited twittering echoed through reception, sending Nancy's mind racing back to the day she arrived. It seemed a lifetime ago.

'Madam?'

The receptionist had dealt with the tourists and stood with a smile inviting her query. Nancy hesitated, her heart trembling as she looked beyond the receptionist to John's closed door. It seemed like a symbol of the direction of her life. There was no way to reach him. Too much lay between them. She shook her head and turned away, choking on the lump in her throat.

Realising she must make arrangements now about where she was to stay for the remainder of her holiday, she stepped on to the terrace to seek Della who was with a group of clients. Nancy waited back until the courier was free. Della gaped, when she saw Nancy.

'Well, I thought you two love birds would be engaging in a fond reunion. Something wrong?'

The smile slipped, replaced by a more sober expression when she noticed Nancy's distress.

'I wondered if you would help me.'

'Whatever is it?'

Della frowned, drawing Nancy away from the constant stream of hotel guests wandering along the path.

'Let's sit over here.'

She led the way to a bench in the shade.

'Have you had a row?'

Nancy shook her head before meeting Della's clear, questioning eyes.

'No . . . well . . . sort of, I suppose. It's a long story. Richard and I broke up, you see, and he now waltzes back into my life and thinks he can pick up the pieces but there's nothing left anymore. I've left him up in my room, but I must find somewhere for myself. I can't share with him under any circumstances.'

'Shall I see if there's another room available?'

'That would be too much fuss. I wondered if I could share with you, just for a couple of nights. I'll keep out of your way. It won't be for long.'

Her eyes were moist, almost luminous as she watched surprise flash on to Della's face. The girl raised her shoulders noncommittally.

'What about asking John.'

'It isn't his concern.'

'You should tell him what's going on.' Della grinned. 'I've noticed he's more than a little distracted by you.'

Nancy shook her head.

'I'll be gone in a couple of days. The distraction will have passed,' she said with finality, biting her lip again as the words provoked more tears to prickle uncomfortably behind her eyelids.

Della was silent, watching Nancy's unease.

'You should think this over. John would want to know. Anyway, bring your stuff up to my room when you're ready. Here's the key. Leave it at reception when you've done.'

She patted Nancy on the shoulder as she made to leave.

'If there's anything else I can do for you, just let me know.'

Nancy sat for a few moments watching Della until she was out of sight. By the fringe of the palms she noticed Kevin, surrounded by a group of giggling girls. His hearty laughter mingled with theirs as he entertained them in his usual carefree manner.

She sighed as she retraced her steps towards the lift. Tensing her shoulders, she cringed at the thought of yet another uneasy confrontation with Richard and as the lift rose, prepared a careful argument designed to counter-act his possible words of persuasion.

Taking a deep breath, she turned the key in the lock and went into the room. Richard was no longer there. She sighed with relief and hurriedly gathered her belongings, throwing them into her suitcase. Then, with a last look

178

around, she left, pulling the door behind her.

Della's room was on the next floor. Nancy ignored the lift and climbed the short flight of stairs, lugging the heavy case. The courier's clothes were strewn around the room, marking her occupancy with a vengeance. Nancy hoisted the case on to the spare bed and selected outfits for the next two days, leaving the rest of her clothes in the suitcase. Like her life, she thought, looking at the untidy pile of creased garments — a complete and utter mess.

She flopped on the bed, covering her face with cupped palms as the floodgate of tears was unleashed. She had got over the heartache of Richard but now there was John. Why didn't I stop it all before it started, was the tormenting thought that haunted her.

Startled by an urgent tapping on the door, Nancy sniffed and dabbed at her cheeks. She glanced in the mirror to see eyes red and puffy from crying in a face that was pale and streaked with distress.

Drawing both hands over her cheeks, she hurried to the door and pulled it open, expecting to see Della. To her dismay it was Richard, his face grim as he held on to his composure, making an obvious effort to appear calm and aloof.

'Look, I've just seen the tour courier. She told me where you were. I've asked her to book me a seat on the next flight home. She's fixed me up and I leave for the airport in a couple of hours.'

A muscle twitched at the corner of his mouth as he went on.

'It wasn't my intention to come to Kenya and ruin what remains of your holiday. You've made it quite clear how you feel. I can't say I blame you, though I was, and am, still willing to make a fresh start.'

He waited, giving Nancy a chance to speak but when she remained silent, he went on.

'Anyway, I never was one to fight over lost causes, so the best thing for both of us is for me to clear off, back to England and out of your life.'

Nancy stood rigidly, biting her lip, as she listened to the words tumbling from Richard's mouth, wondering if this was the prelude to another plea for them to start again. When he looked at her intently, his eyes asked for some response and she swallowed hard before speaking.

'It's for the best Richard,' she said in a wavering voice she fought to control. 'The best for both of us. Too much has happened for it ever to be the same again. I think we should cut our losses and go our own way.'

'OK, then, if that's what you truly want. Let's get your things back to your own room.'

He pushed past her into Della's apartment and waited until Nancy shoved her clothes back in the suitcase. Picking it up, he led the way down the stairs with Nancy following a few steps behind. She was still apprehensive until Richard unlocked the door to her room. His luggage was lined up inside. Nancy glanced at it and turned to smile.

'You really meant what you said.'

181

With genuine relief, she leaned forward to kiss him on the cheek.

'Thank you, Richard.'

At that moment, glancing over his shoulder, she saw John stepping out of the lift with the doors slowly closing behind him! His eyes were filled with undisguised anger as he glared with a malevolent hatred. Nancy noticed the clenched fists at his side, thumping against his thigh in a regular beat.

He caught the lift door before it shut and wrenched it open. Turning on his heel, he stepped back inside, staring bitterly until the doors finally closed. The brief respite from despair that had begun with Richard's acceptance of the situation was over. Nancy's heart plummeted. She barely heard the drone of Richard's words. It was only when he tapped her arm that she was able to focus on the present.

'I have a little over an hour to kill before I leave for the airport. Let's have a drink for old time's sake. Come on.'

Nancy nodded. Moving to the door

in a bewildered gaze, she followed him downstairs to sit at a table on the terrace. She watched Richard cross the lawns to the bar. His tall, erect figure in grey slacks and pale blue shirt stood out among the less soberly clad holiday makers. She smiled weakly, noticing how he turned his head to follow the progress of a bronzed sunbather in a tiny bikini. Richard would be over their final parting sooner than he thought!

As for herself, Nancy knew that John would be in her heart and mind whenever she thought of Kenya. Each lonely moment would be filled with memories of his kisses. But they were worlds apart. John, too, would forget her in no time. Her heart drained of emotion and felt numb inside her chest as she watched Richard return with the drinks.

The glasses were drained and conversation dwindling to uneasy silences by the time Della gathered together the passengers due to leave for the airport.

Richard stood and gathered his jacket and flight bag before bending to kiss Nancy on the cheek. His look of regret was tinged with a hint of relief to be on his way.

'No hard feelings, Nancy,' he said offering his hand.

When Nancy left him, mounting the steps of the bus, she knew that a chapter of her life had finally ended. She turned back into the foyer, resigned to wait out the time for her own departure as stoically as she could. Pressing the call button of the lift Nancy waited for it to arrive. As she opened the door to her room a deep sigh escaped as she wished that she, too, was on the way home. The next few days would be difficult. John had made his feelings clear. It was obvious he no longer had anything to say to her. His infatuation was over.

Sitting in the familiar surroundings of her room, where so recently she had experienced the joy of getting ready to meet him, Nancy felt the loneliness close around her like an icy blanket blotting out the heat. Remembering the bouquet of frangipani blossoms that had filled the room with sweetness, her eyes misted, knowing the joy had gone from her life more quickly than the flowers had faded. Nothing would ever be the same again.

There was a rapid knocking outside. Her stomach knotted and her shoulders grew tense as the tapping continued. A thought crossed her mind with a pang of apprehension. It couldn't be Richard! Had he forgotten something? Or had he changed his mind? Anxiously, she hurried across the room and tugged the door open.

'John!'

He leaned against the door post looking at her sternly, both hands shoved into his trouser pockets.

'What the devil are you playing at?' he demanded.

Nancy was disturbed by his tone. She glared into his face, waiting for him to explain his outburst.

'What is going on?' he was almost yelling at her. 'Why didn't you come to me, Nancy, and tell me what was happening? Don't I mean anything to you at all? I know Richard has gone,' he added, lowering his voice.

Nancy backed into the room and went to the window, reluctant to meet his eyes.

'I'll be gone, too, in a couple of days,' she repeated. 'It'll be all over. It could never work between us.'

'My love, if you're not happy here, we'll go back to England, anywhere, just as long as we're together. I'm not going to let you out of my life.'

'We hardly know each other,' she cried through a voice strained with emotion and amazement. 'You should choose someone who would fit in with your life. It's best we say goodbye.'

'And is this what you want, Nancy? Just tell me you never want to see me again and I'll leave, right now.'

He was silent, waiting for her to speak, but the words bubbled in her mouth. She didn't know what to say. How could she send him away? But even more difficult, how could she keep him?

John swore under his breath and Nancy winced as his fist hammered the wall. She heard the door bang and glanced at the picture above the dressing-table as it shuddered with the violent tremor.

He had gone. Her heart lurched with the pain of final separation. But suddenly she was seized from behind by two strong arms that spun her round, almost toppling her from her feet.

'Don't you listen to anything I say? I love you, Nancy. We have a future together, here in Kenya. Just say the word. We have all the time in the world ahead of us to get to know each other. I have never been more sure of anything than I am right now. You're the one with whom I want to spend the rest of my life.'

Nancy gasped through a daze that was constricting the breath in her lungs.

The nearness of him was intoxicating her senses to a pitch where she knew she was about to surrender. She would go anywhere with him, stay with him, be with him. He was all she wanted and he was here.

He kissed her with an urgency that caused her heart to thud, pounding out its beat in a rapid tattoo. Her limbs weakened against him as she felt the heat from his body fuse against her own.

His mouth moved over her cheek and rested briefly on her eyelids before finding her lips. Her mouth felt bruised under his onslaught but she barely noticed the discomfort as she wound her arms tightly around his neck, pulling him closer as she melted into his arms.

As if the torrent was released and spent, he eased his face away to look into her eyes, stroking her hair with gentle fingers.

'I'll never let you go. We'll make it work. When you leave here, you'll be coming to Kericho with me, and I won't take no for an answer, Nancy. It has to be yes.'

Nancy found his lips again, now moist and cool when she kissed him. The gloom of the past had faded in the heat of their passion and the future opened up like a pathway leading into the sunlight. Their love erupted like frangipani blossoms, filling their senses with the sweetness of life.

'Yes ... yes ... yes ... ' she murmured.

THE END

We do hope that you have enjoyed reading this large print book.

Did you know that all of our titles are available for purchase?

We publish a wide range of high quality large print books including:
Romances, Mysteries, Classics
General Fiction
Non Fiction and Westerns

Special interest titles available in large print are:
The Little Oxford Dictionary
Music Book, Song Book
Hymn Book, Service Book

Also available from us courtesy of Oxford University Press:
Young Readers' Dictionary
(large print edition)
Young Readers' Thesaurus
(large print edition)

For further information or a free brochure, please contact us at:
Ulverscroft Large Print Books Ltd.,
The Green, Bradgate Road, Anstey,
Leicester, LE7 7FU, England.
Tel: (00 44) **0116 236 4325**
Fax: (00 44) **0116 234 0205**

VISIONS OF THE HEART

Christine Briscomb

When property developer Connor
Grant contracted Natalie Jensen to
landscape the grounds of his large
country house near Ashley in South
Australia, she was ecstatic. But then
she discovered he was acquiring
— and ripping apart — great
swathes of the town. Her own
mother's house and the hall where
the drama group met were two of his
targets. Natalie was desperate to
stop Connor's plans — but she also
had to fight the powerful attraction
flowing between them.

FINGALA, MAID OF RATHAY

Mary Cummins

On his deathbed, Sir James Montgomery of Rathay asks his daughter, Fingala, to swear that she will not honour her marriage contract until her brother Patrick, the new heir, returns from serving the King. Patrick must marry. Rathay must not be left without a mistress. But Patrick has fallen in love with the Lady Catherine Gordon whom the King, James IV, has given in marriage to the young man who claims to be Richard of York, one of the princes in the Tower.

ZABILLET OF THE SNOW

Catherine Darby

For Zabillet, a young peasant girl growing up in the tiny French village of Fromage in the mid-fourteenth century, a respectable marriage is the height of her parents' ambitions for her. But life is changing. Zabillet's love for a handsome shepherd is tested when she is invited to join the La Neige household, where her mistress, Lady Petronella, has plans for her grandson, Benet. And over all broods the horror of the Great Death that claims all whom it touches.

PERILOUS JOURNEY

Caroline Joyce

After the execution of Charles I, Louisa's Royalist father considers it too dangerous for her to stay in England and arranges for her to go to the Isle of Man with Armand de la Tremouille, the nephew of the island's Royalist Governor. Their ship is boarded by Parliamentarians who plan to sail for Ireland, but a storm causes them to be shipwrecked on the Calf of Man. Magnus Stapleton, the Parliamentarian chief, becomes infatuated with Louisa, but she has fallen in love with Armand.